NURSE ON SKIS

Kay is delighted to be back in Scotland. A new job — district nurse — is waiting, and her boss is her uncle, Dr. Edgar Duncan, a GP in Stranduthie. Excited about her new life and the challenge of covering three villages in a remote area, she quickly settles into a routine. Dr. Clive Farrell, her uncle's new partner in the practice, soon falls for her, and she feels attracted to him as well. The path of true love runs smoothly until Dr. Frank Munro arrives, seemingly intent on ruining Kay's dream . . .

PHYLLIS MALLETT

◆

NURSE
ON SKIS

Complete and Unabridged

LINFORD
Leicester

First published in Great Britain in 1972

First Linford Edition
published 2017

A catalogue record for this book is available
from the British Library.

ISBN 978–1–4448–3508–3

Published by
F. A. Thorpe (Publishing)
Anstey, Leicestershire

Set by Words & Graphics Ltd.
Anstey, Leicestershire
Printed and bound in Great Britain by
T. J. International Ltd., Padstow, Cornwall

This book is printed on acid-free paper

1

It was directly after Christmas that Kay Whittaker left London to take up the position of district nurse in the remote part of Western Scotland where her uncle, Dr. Edgar Duncan, had his general practice. She had no regrets, as she sat in the train taking her north, and she looked forward to starting the New Year with a new life. There was nothing left for her in London. As a nurse in a large general hospital, she had been merely a cog in a large machine. It had suited her at first to remain anonymous, but deep down inside she had been chafing because of the way life seemed to be passing her by.

Kay's face softened as she thought of her aunt and uncle, who had taken an interest in her ever since her own parents had been killed in an aeroplane crash. They had always welcomed her warmly on her regular visits to their home in Stranduthie, and Kay knew that Edgar Duncan had pulled several strings to get her the job as district nurse. She leant back in her seat and thought about what lay ahead of her.

The work involved would be completely different from that to which she was accustomed, and probably a good deal harder. There were three villages in the district which she had been allocated, and that would mean a large area to cover. Nevertheless, Kay refused to be daunted — she looked forward to the challenge with excitement and enthusiasm . . .

Scotland had always attracted her, Kay admitted to herself some hours later, when they were passing through the lowlands. She had changed trains at Edinburgh, and was now being carried to the west and north. In the past she had always been excited by this part of the journey; but then she had been travelling on holiday, and this time there would be no going back.

She pictured the little town of Stranduthie, and in her mind she could see the distant mountains, the wide moors, the little villages clustered here and there among the rough countryside. She would not be disappointed with what awaited her, she knew. Her mother had lived in these parts during a very happy childhood, and her Aunt Margaret looked enough like her mother to make her feel very much at home.

Kay arrived at the little station in Stranduthie during darkness, and alighted from the local train with a great sigh of relief. The platform was dimly lit, and she looked around anxiously for her uncle. When she failed to spot his short, dumpy figure, her heart missed a beat and she had to fight the unexpected desire to cry. Suddenly, she felt very lonely, though she could not have said why. After all, there had been nothing and no one to keep her in London.

A porter appeared and helped her with her luggage. The heavier cases had been sent on ahead, but she had three suitcases with her, and two of them were very heavy indeed. They walked along the platform, and Kay anxiously scanned the faces waiting at the ticket barrier, but she failed to see her uncle, who had promised in a letter to be waiting for her on her arrival.

As they went through the barrier, Kay began to think of taking a taxi. Her uncle's house was on the far side of the town, and Kay could already feel the cold night seeping into her bones. Then a tall figure stepped in front of her, and she paused and looked up into a shadowed face.

'Excuse me,' the man said, 'but are you Kay Whittaker?'

'I am!' She spoke eagerly. So she hadn't been forgotten! No doubt Uncle Edgar was out on a case.

'I'm sorry you have to be met by a total stranger, but your uncle was called out on an emergency, and he asked me to collect you. I'm Clive Farrell, your uncle's new partner. You heard about the death of old Dr. Jameson, didn't you?'

'Yes. It was sad. I knew Dr. Jameson quite well. So you have taken his place!' Kay looked up at her companion, trying to see what he looked like, but he was wearing a big overcoat with the collar turned up.

He took two of her cases, and Kay walked behind him as he turned on his heel to leave the station. She shivered as they reached the street, and to her surprise she found snow falling quite heavily, covering everything in a thin white blanket. Clive Farrell stowed her cases in the boot of a near-by car, then opened a door for her, and Kay sighed with relief as she got into the vehicle and settled down.

She looked into his face as he got into the car, for the interior light was on, and she found him surveying her. She smiled as their glances met, and she saw that he was young — no more than thirty — and that he was fairish haired and very handsome. He smiled at her, showing perfect teeth, and he paused to shake some of the snow off his shoulders before settling into his seat.

'You've picked the wrong time of the year to come up here,' he commented as he started the car. 'It's going to be a tough job for you, trying to get around to the villages during the snow and the bad weather.'

'I know Nurse Harmon's been doing the job. In fact, she's done it for years,' Kay said. 'But she's retiring at the end of the year — this week, in fact — and if she could do it, then I'm sure I shall manage.'

Clive nodded, and Kay watched him furtively as he drove carefully through what was rapidly becoming a blizzard. He glanced at her when he was forced to stop at some traffic lights, and she could see his face quite plainly.

'I feel as if I know you quite well,' he said slowly. 'I have been told quite a lot about you in the time that I've been with your uncle. I'm living at your uncle's house, by the way. I hope I shan't be in your way.'

'Why should you be?' Kay smiled. 'There's enough room in that big old house for a dozen doctors.'

'Your uncle thought it would be better for me to live in and be on hand,' he went on. 'The arrangement has worked rather well so far, but if I do get in your way, then don't hesitate to let me know.'

She studied his profile as he went on, and found herself liking him.

'Thank you for turning out,' she said, and shivered as she peered ahead through the windscreen. Snow was falling thickly, and she was thankful that the interior of the car was well heated. 'It isn't fit to turn a dog out tonight, is it?'

'It isn't fit for anyone to be out, except doctors,' he replied with a chuckle.

Kay laughed and felt her former

loneliness disappearing as quickly as it had come; she relaxed in her seat, soothed by the friendly atmosphere in the car. Perhaps she dozed because, in what seemed no time at all, they had drawn up in front of her uncle's house. Kay got up hurriedly from her seat, eager to see her aunt again.

'Go on into the house and I'll bring in your cases,' Clive Farrell said, and she thanked him for his understanding and hurried along the path to the house.

Her aunt must have been watching for her arrival, for the door opened as she reached it, and the next instant Kay was enveloped in her aunt's arms. They kissed affectionately, and when they drew apart, Kay was studied very closely by Margaret Duncan's cool brown eyes.

'I'm thankful you've arrived, Kay,' the older woman said in warm tones. 'I've been worried in case you changed your mind at the last minute. But you're here now and, although it isn't the best time of the year to start your new job, the worst of the weather will be over by the time you've settled in.'

Kay looked into her aunt's happy face and knew that her own face mirrored the other's happiness. She wanted so much to belong and her aunt was the only person in the world now to whom she could turn for understanding and advice. Margaret Duncan was small and thin, with a gentle face which showed the years of service she had given to the sick — she had been a nurse before marrying Edgar Duncan.

'Aunt, you can't know how happy I am to be here,' Kay said, smiling. 'I must admit that I was a little dubious at first about leaving London, but now that I'm here, I know that I have made the right decision. I can hardly wait to start my new job!'

Margaret Duncan laughed, then turned as Clive Farrell came into the room with Kay's suitcases.

'I'll take these straight up to Kay's room, shall I?' he demanded.

'Please do, Clive,' Margaret said. 'I hope you two will get along well together.'

'We're sure to,' he replied, his brown eyes twinkling as he looked at Kay. 'I'm not the quarrelsome type, and I don't suppose we shall have time to get bored with each other, duty being what it is.'

He put down the cases and looked seriously into Kay's face, and she felt colour seeping into her cheeks for some unaccountable reason. His bold gaze seemed to confuse her, and she had to make an effort to remain calm before him. 'I don't know how you're going to manage to get around your district,' he said. 'I have spoken to your uncle about this. You won't be able to use a cycle in the snow, and when the drifts get really deep a car will be out of the question. Do you drive, by the way?'

'I've had a driving licence for about five years,' Kay said, smiling. 'But I haven't done much driving in the past year or two.'

He nodded slowly. 'I'll give you some

lessons if you wish. You may need a refresher course, especially if the snow keeps falling — but we'll talk more about it when you've rested. It's been a long journey from London, hasn't it?'

'I didn't notice, really,' she confessed. 'I read or dozed most of the time.'

Aunt Margaret took her arm and led her into the large front sitting-room. Kay looked around with interest.

'You've decorated since I was last here,' she observed. 'I like this! It's so much cosier, Aunt! Who helped you do it? I'm sure Uncle didn't.'

'No.' Margaret Duncan shook her head, a smile on her face. 'Edgar hasn't the time or the inclination for decorating. Clive helped me choose the paper. Do you like his taste?'

'I do.' Kay nodded emphatically. 'It makes something of the room now!'

'Flattery will get you everywhere!' said Clive's voice behind them, and Kay turned to meet his laughing eyes.

'It wasn't flattery,' she admonished, 'it was the unvarnished truth. But when did you find the time to do it, Clive?'

'We do get free time, sometimes, you know,' he said cheerfully. 'I like doing this sort of thing, anyway, and it helped pass the time when I wasn't on call.'

'Clive has done your bedroom, too, Kay, and I think we'd better go up and look at it. If you don't like the paper he chose, then he'll start again.'

'I'm very easy to please where that sort of thing is concerned,' Kay said.

'That's a relief,' he retorted. 'I've been worried in case all my efforts were in vain.'

They left the sitting-room and went up to Kay's bedroom, and she turned to Clive when she saw the pretty wallpaper he had selected for her. It was of a white background with sprays of red and pink roses patterned upon it.

'I wouldn't have chosen anything else if I'd seen this one in the shop,' she said.

He nodded, smiling. 'Thank you again for being so kind,' he said.

Aunt Margaret was pleased, and she

impulsively hugged Kay, who put an affectionate arm round the older woman.

'Everything is going to be all right,' Aunt Margaret said. 'I can feel it in my bones.'

A voice called up to them from the hall and Kay turned instantly, recognizing her uncle's tones. She hurried from the room and descended the stairs, to throw herself rather boisterously into his arms.

'Kay, I'm so happy to see you, my dear. I'm sorry I couldn't get to the station, but Clive is an able chap, and I'm sure he took great care of you.'

'Yes, thank you, Uncle,' she replied, pushing away from him in order to look into his weathered face. 'I'm so glad to see you again, too.' She paused as she surveyed him, and a frown touched her smooth forehead. 'You're looking tired and strained,' she said sharply. 'You're not doing too much, are you?'

'No more than usual, my dear.' His blue eyes beamed for a moment. He was a medium-sized man, rather stocky, and his grey hair made him look distinguished. 'I suppose I'm beginning to feel my age. I can well remember the time when I could get my work finished and find the energy to follow my hobbies, but now I'm lucky if I can keep my eyes open after getting home.'

She nodded slowly, linking an arm through his, and they faced the stairs as Margaret Duncan descended, followed by Clive.

'Thank you for meeting Kay, Clive,' Edgar said. 'Come and have a drink, eh?' He spoke in well modulated tones which gave very little indication of his Scottish origin. Some words he used, however, had an unmistakable burr to them and, for as long as she could remember, Kay had loved to listen to his speech.

They went back into the sitting-room, and Aunt Margaret attended to the drinks. Kay had a sherry and Clive a whisky, but Edgar asked for brandy, and Kay sat watching him intently during the next few minutes while they all chatted generally. She didn't like the look of strain that clung to her uncle's face, and his pale blue eyes seemed to show a great deal of heavy weariness.

The telephone rang in the hall, and Clive hastened in answer. When he returned his face was showing concern.

'It's from the Kilpatrick household,' he announced. 'Old James has taken a turn for the worse.'

'I'd better go and see him immediately.' Edgar pushed himself to his feet with a sigh. 'I looked in on him this morning and rather fancied that he would deteriorate.'

'Shall I go instead?' Clive demanded. 'You're looking very tired, Edgar, and I have been treating James Kilpatrick.'

'I'm on call,' Edgar said stubbornly. 'When I can't make my own calls I shall retire.'

Kay was a little surprised by the sharpness of her uncle's tones, and she glanced at Clive's face. But there was no expression showing on the younger

15

man's features, though when she turned her eyes to Aunt Margaret, she found the woman watching her husband rather critically. Edgar set down his glass and excused himself, going out to the hall to put on his overcoat.

'Are you hungry, Kay?' Aunt Margaret demanded. 'I can get you something if you'd like a meal.'

'I am rather hungry,' Kay said. 'But don't do anything special for me. I can wait until supper time if you wish.'

'Nonsense! I'll get you some soup. You sit here and talk to Clive, while I make it.'

The older woman left the room and Kay turned her attention to Clive Farrell.

'I don't think my uncle is very well, Clive,' she said slowly. 'Is he doing too much?'

'I'm afraid he is.' Clive shook his head as he considered. 'Your aunt and I have been trying to relieve him of some of the strain, but you know your uncle. He'll do his fair share of the work even if it kills him — which it is quite likely to do if he doesn't begin to ease up.'

'What do you mean?' Kay's eyes were wide as she studied his serious expression.

'Your uncle is sick, Kay. He's been doing too much for too many years and he's suffering from a heart condition. But he's like an old war horse which scents battle and must join in. Your aunt and I have been trying to get him to slow down, but it isn't any use. He's going to continue working at his present pace until he drops.'

'I could see the strain in his face as soon as he came through the door,' Kay said. 'Uncle Edgar is nearly sixty-seven and well past retirement age. But I really can't see him wanting to retire yet. However, we must do something to make him take a rest now and then.'

'And before it is too late,' he said, nodding. 'Your aunt has been counting the days to your arrival, for she says you can persuade your uncle to do things where even she fails. We'll have to work together against him in the hope that our combined efforts will prevail, although I don't hold out much hope. He's a strong-minded man and he's going to fight us all the way.'

* * *

In the following three days, Kay found herself accepting naturally the changes which were taking place in her life. While in London she had feared that she would not be able to settle down in Stranduthie, but now she realized that she had been foolish to worry.

Perhaps Clive Farrell helped a great deal, for she spent a considerable time in his company. He asked her to make the rounds with him the day after her arrival, ostensibly to show her where her own work would take her, and Kay accompanied him afterwards whenever he was called out during the day in order to consolidate the knowledge she was gaining. She found herself coming to like Clive Farrell almost without realizing it. He was a cheerful man, and joked incessantly, drawing her into his laughter and getting her into the same mood. She found herself light-hearted and gay, even when they were caught in snowdrifts on the way to see patients.

As the new district nurse, Kay came under the control of the local Health Department, and made it her business to report to them as soon as possible. Then she went to see the district nurse whose place she was taking: Nurse Harmon. Her knock at the nurse's door was answered by a small, silver-haired woman, and Kay held out her hand eagerly.

'Nurse Harmon, it's so nice to see you again. How are you keeping?'

'Kay Whittaker!' The older woman's gentle face was creased by a wide smile. 'Do come in out of the snow. I was hoping you would come and see me before taking up your duties. I expect there is quite a lot I can tell you.'

'That's why I've come to see you, Nurse.' Kay stamped the snow from her boots before crossing the threshold. 'I hope you're going to enjoy your retirement.' She smiled as she was helped out of her coat. 'You've been the district nurse around here for as long as I can remember.'

'I shall be sad at making the break, and I shall find it difficult to accept the fact that there will be no more calls for me in the middle of the night,' said Nurse Harmon, wistfully. 'Still, I'm pleased that it's you who is taking over from me, Kay. Perhaps you will let me come out with you on your rounds from time to time, then I shan't feel my retirement so keenly?'

'Of course. I'd love to have you with me,' Kay said instantly. 'How do you make your rounds, Nurse? Do you have a car?'

'A car is supplied by the Department,' Nurse Harmon said. 'The district I cover is so very large, a car is imperative. I handle the three villages of Cairnburn, Brecknockie and Kilbernian, and it's a long day to get around them in turn, then to go out on emergency calls. There's a midwife in town here, to take care of that side of the business, but you are responsible for births in the villages, and no doubt you'll discover, as I did, that babies pick the most awkward times to be born!'

'I shan't mind,' Kay said, her eyes shining with expectation. 'I can't wait to take over from you, Nurse. But perhaps I can make the rounds with you on the next three days in order to get used to the calls. It was suggested at the Department when I visited them this morning.'

'Of course. I shall look forward to showing you around,' came the immediate reply. 'I've finished for the day now, except for emergency calls, of course, so perhaps you would like a cup of tea? I was about to put the kettle on when you knocked.'

'That would be lovely,' Kay said, and followed the other woman into the small but spotless kitchen. While Nurse Harmon made the tea, they chatted generally about the duties Kay would be required to fulfil in her new job.

Kay stayed with Nurse Harmon for more than an hour, listening to advice and taking it in. They made arrangements for Kay to go with the older nurse on her round the following morning, and when she departed, Kay took with her a wealth of information which was the result of Nurse Harmon's long experience.

Kay walked thoughtfully back towards her uncle's house, trying to remember and absorb as much of what the other woman had told her as she could. There were so many details that Kay knew it would be some time before she was quite sure of them all; however, knowledge comes with experience and she found herself keener than ever to begin work.

The sound of a car drawing up at the kerb beside her startled her out of her reverie, and she looked up to recognize it as Clive's. She smiled when she saw him geting out of his seat with his medical bag in his hand.

'Hello!' he said. 'You're looking pleased with yourself. What have you been up to today?'

'It will take too long to tell you in detail,' she teased. 'Are you still on your rounds?'

'I am, but this is the last call, unless there have been any emergencies in the last hour or so. I'll ring the house before returning.'

'May I wait for you, if this is your last call?'

'Please do! Sit in the car. It's warmer in there. I shan't be very long. This is just a routine visit.'

She nodded and got into the car, and watched him as he went to a near-by house. Unconsciously, she smiled as she thought of him. There was a great deal about Clive which attracted her: he thought the same way as she did; he had pleasant manners and an abundance of charm; and, of course, he was very good-looking, even when he wore his glasses. Privately, Kay loved to see

Clive in his glasses — they gave him an air of distinction and quiet confidence . . .

She was still thinking about him when he returned to the car, and Kay realized that her blue eyes were shining as she looked at him. He smiled in his usual cheerful fashion as he got behind the wheel, and then paused in the action of starting the engine to take in her flushed face and brightly gleaming eyes.

'You look as if you've had some good news,' he said. 'What have you been doing today?'

'I've been talking with Nurse Harmon. I take over from her on Sunday — Saturday evening, actually — and she's been putting me in the picture. I'm going to make the rounds with her tomorrow, and probably on Friday and Saturday as well. Then I shall know exactly what it is I've got to do and what will be expected of me.'

'You're my idea of a dedicated nurse,' he said softly. 'But you're going to find that your life will be one long succession of hurrying around the villages at everyone's beck and call.'

'I shan't mind that so long as I'm helping the sick,' she retorted, and he nodded slowly.

'You're half-way to succeeding in this job before you start,' he mused. 'But make up your mind to the fact that it's going to be very difficult during the winter.'

'You've mentioned that before,' she said. 'Why should it be very difficult, Clive?'

He sighed rather heavily before attempting to reply, and Kay watched his face intently. His dark eyes were narrowed as he stared through the windscreen at the snowy scene before them.

'There's a lot more snow to come,' he said. 'Your uncle has told me countless tales of having to struggle through all obstacles to reach a patient's bedside, and you can see what the efforts over the years have done to your uncle.

You're going to have to face similar strains, Kay.'

'Well, I'm young and strong, and I've always been noted for my determination.' She smiled. 'I like a challenge, you know. I shall look forward to battling against the elements.'

He laughed, shaking his head as he looked at her. But there was respect in his expression, and she was pleased to see it there in his handsome face. She took a deep breath and tried to control the unexpected surge of emotion within her. She wasn't at all sure that she wanted this man to have such an effect on her, especially when they were still comparative strangers.

'Are you in a hurry to get home?' Clive asked abruptly.

'Not in the least. Is there somewhere you want to go before returning?'

'I was wondering if you'd like to come for a short drive with me. The main roads aren't too bad today — salt has been spread on them — and it would be nice to get away from

26

everything for a short time.'

'I'd like that very much,' Kay said warmly.

'Good,' said Clive, and started the car. He concentrated upon his driving until he was clear of the deeper snow at the kerbside, then he followed the roads until they reached the town's limits, and Kay saw that the road ahead was fairly clear of snow. They went on at a slightly faster rate, and she leaned back in her seat and sighed heavily.

'What do you really make of Uncle Edgar?' she demanded, suddenly turning towards Clive.

'I think he's got to ease up considerably or he may not see the winter through.'

'Is it as bad as that?' Her eyes widened as she stared at him.

'I think so, but every time I try to talk about his health, your uncle shuts me up, or retreats before I can say anything constructive.'

'That's what I would expect him to do!' Kay held her breath for a moment, then exhaled sharply. She narrowed her eyes as she stared ahead into the swirling snow. 'Have you told Aunt Margaret exactly what your fears are?'

'No!' He shook his head emphatically. 'I thought it better to keep quiet about it. I knew you were coming, and I imagined you would know what to do.'

'I must confess that I'm at a loss,' she said, shaking her head. 'I know Uncle would resist any move to limit his duties and, in any case, you couldn't take on the work he didn't do. What is really needed is a locum while he takes a holiday.'

'He needs quite a long holiday!'

Kay thought that over for some moments, and found that she didn't like the sound of it. If Uncle Edgar needed a long holiday, then he really must be in quite a serious condition.

'I think I'll have a talk with Uncle himself,' she said at length. 'I might be able to talk some sense into him.'

'Perhaps it might be better to acquaint your aunt with the facts and persuade her to put some pressure on him!' Clive shook his head. 'I just don't know what to do for the best.'

'Aunt was a nurse, you know, so she's well able to handle any emergency, and she isn't the kind to break down and cry at the news. I think she should be told. She has a right to know.'

'I'll tell her as soon as we get home,' Clive said. 'I'm glad you've helped me to reach a decision.'

'You really are sure that Uncle's as bad as you say he is, Clive?' Kay asked.

'As sure as I can be on the scant evidence that I have. Of course, he wouldn't let me examine him, so I can't produce any real evidence; but it's fairly easy to see that the job has become too much for him. We need another partner!'

'Would that settle the problem? If Uncle did take things a little easier, would his condition mend?'

'It would certainly improve, there's no doubt about that. If he could cut down on his rounds, then all would be well. But he drives himself to his limit, and that's not good.'

'He's always done that!' Kay shook her head slowly. 'I don't think he could work in any other way.'

Clive slowed the car and turned it carefully, avoiding the deeper drifts of snow at the side of the road. When they were facing back the way they had come, he opened his door and got out. Kay looked at him, inquiringly.

'You can drive us back,' he said. 'You're going to need some practice before you start your rounds on Sunday.'

With a rueful smile, Kay nodded and slipped across into the driving seat. When Clive had got into the other seat, she set off, determined to show how well she could manage, but the car skidded first to one side of the road and then to the other while she was still in the lower gears. She drove gingerly, her nerves taut, but the higher gears enabled the wheels to turn without skidding, and they went back to town without mishap. Once in the town, with the main road relatively dry after salt had melted the snow, Kay found it quite simple to drive, and she told herself that, if they didn't get much more snow than was already lying around, she would not be very severely tested this winter.

'You did all right,' Clive told her as she finally brought the car to a halt outside the house. 'I was really quite impressed!'

Kay smiled impishly. 'To quote your own words: 'Flattery will get you everywhere'.'

When they entered the house, Kay sought out her aunt, and she found the older woman in the front sitting-room reading a magazine.

'Hello, Kay, where have you been? I expected you back some time ago!'

'Anything wrong, Aunt?'

'No! I just wondered where you could be.'

Kay explained her activities, and she saw a twinkle come into Margaret

Duncan's eyes at mention of the drive she had taken with Clive. Kay smiled as she read her aunt's mind, but she didn't want to give rise to any speculation. She had something most serious to relate, and didn't relish the task. However, the sooner her aunt knew about Edgar's condition, the sooner they could try to do something about it.

'Aunt, I've been having a most serious talk with Clive,' she began, wondering how to lead up to the disclosure. She hesitated for a few moments, until Margaret Duncan cut in impatiently.

'What's troubling you, Kay?' the older woman demanded. 'You can tell me, surely!'

'I can, Aunt, although I'd like to spare you the worry.' Kay steeled herself, then began to relate what had passed between herself and Clive. She told her aunt the bare facts, and could see by the woman's reaction that it came as no great surprise. When she lapsed into silence, Margaret Duncan nodded slowly.

'I've known about your uncle's condition for quite some time now, Kay,' she said sadly, 'although I didn't know it was as bad as Clive thinks. However, I have been of the opinion that Edgar would suffer more if his duties were curtailed than he is suffering at the moment. That's why I've done nothing about him. He would worry so much if he felt he wasn't doing his fair share.'

'I appreciate your feelings, Aunt,' Kay said thinly, her voice tight with suppressed emotion. 'But you're going to lose him if he doesn't cut down. Clive thinks he may not see the winter through.'

'Surely not!' Panic showed on Margaret Duncan's calm face, but was quickly mastered and controlled. 'Then we must put our heads together and make some plan of action.'

'We must,' Kay said gently, and she sat down at her aunt's side and put an affectionate arm around the older woman's shoulder. 'We'll do what we can, Aunt, don't you worry — and it will be all right, I'm sure!'

2

The next day dawned gloomy and cold, and Kay felt apprehensive when she looked from the window while waiting for Nurse Harmon to come and pick her up. Snow clouds were thick and heavy overhead, and already the crisp air was filled with flying flakes. There had been a snow-fall during the night, and the path showed an unbroken surface to her blue eyes.

'Will you have another cup of tea before you go, Kay?' Aunt Margaret demanded.

'No thank you, Aunt. I've had quite sufficient to help keep out the cold. If I can't face the weather today, then I shall never be able to.'

Kay saw a car draw up at the gate, and watched Nurse Harmon alight. The older woman picked her way through the deeper snow at the kerb and came through the gateway. Kay went to the door to greet her.

'If you're ready, Kay, we'll make an early start,' the older woman said. 'I think the roads are going to be difficult today.'

'I've been ready for quite some time,' Kay replied, and turned to call good-bye to her aunt before following Nurse Harmon outside.

When they were seated in the car, Nurse Harmon turned to Kay. The interior of the vehicle was warm, and Kay relaxed a little.

'I always drive into Cairnburn first,' Nurse Harmon said. 'I like to work in that direction and come back to town through Brechnockie and Kilbernian. Usually I get through the three villages by noon, and in the afternoon there are clinics to attend and various classes for young or expectant mothers.'

Kay nodded, bringing her attention to bear upon the woman's words, for she knew she could not afford to overlook any advice which might be forthcoming from this experienced woman.

When they reached the outskirts of the town they found the roads worse. There were patches of ice hidden under the thin layer of treacherous snow which had fallen, and Nurse Harmon drove at a speed of about twenty miles per hour in order to avoid skidding; nevertheless the rear end of the car swayed alarmingly at times.

'It's not too bad today,' Nurse Harmon remarked at length, and Kay glanced at the woman's serene face, wondering if she were joking; but the older woman smiled as she glanced at Kay. 'It's the deep snow that causes most trouble,' she elucidated. 'But you'll discover that for yourself before winter is done.'

Kay nodded without comment, gazing around at the frozen countryside as they went on. They eventually reached Cairn-burn, a rather large village some seven miles from Stranduthie, in about twice the time it should normally have taken them. Nurse Harmon halted the car in the park beside the small public house, and they alighted.

'Jamie Lyons, the publican, fell down the steps of his cellar three weeks ago, and he wouldn't stay in hospital. He broke his right arm and suffered bad lacerations, which I'm still treating. His arm is in plaster, of course, but Jamie is a very bad patient!'

Nurse Harmon led the way to the side door of the building, and a dog set up a ferocious barking when she knocked. A tall, thin woman with a tired face and thick grey hair opened the door to them, but her features brightened as she smiled a welcome.

'Come in, Nurse,' she said cheerfully. 'I was just saying to Jamie that we should be lucky to see you today, but it would take a blizzard to keep you from your patients, I suspect.'

'That it would, Mrs. Lyons,' the old nurse replied. 'I have a companion today.' She turned and smiled at Kay as they entered the house. 'This is Nurse

Whittaker, and she's taking over from me when I retire on Saturday. You'll probably know her uncle, Dr. Duncan.'

'Of course!' Mrs. Lyons held out a ready hand. 'I'm very pleased to meet you, Nurse Whittaker. It will be a sad day for us when Nurse Harmon does give up, but we shall make her successor welcome.'

Nurse Harmon smiled as they went through the house to a large sitting-room, where they found a heavily-built, grey-haired man seated by a blazing log fire. His right arm was in a sling and there were plasters on his face and on his left hand. He looked up at their entrance, and smiled broadly.

'You're a sight for sore eyes,' he declared, and stared curiously at Kay, who was not in uniform. She was introduced to Jamie Lyons, who motioned to his broken arm with a sad expression on his weathered face. 'So you're to be the new nurse, eh?' he continued, studying her face. 'And you're Dr. Duncan's niece! That makes you one of us, and there'll be a great many people who'll take to you because of it. I wish you well, but you'll find it a terrible job, in the present conditions.'

'It hasn't been too bad so far,' Nurse Harmon said. She set down her bag and took off her gloves, going to stand by the fire to warm her hands before touching the patient.

Kay watched while Nurse Harmon removed the old dressings from Jamie Lyons's face and hand, replacing them with new ones. She was impressed by the way the older woman soothed and relaxed her patient by a flow of easy chatter, and knew that she would have to work very hard indeed to measure up to Nurse Harmon's standards. She said as much when they went back to the car after their work had been finished, and was glad to see the pleased flush which touched Nurse Harmon's cheeks.

When they left the village, after visiting the other patients there, and started on the four-mile drive to Brechnockie, the snow was really pouring down, and it was difficult for Nurse Harmon to see through the windscreen. A fine layer of snow covered the car and stuck to the windscreen despite the efforts of the wipers. Nurse Harmon eventually stopped by the side of the road, and left the engine running while they waited for the worst of the flurry to end.

'It looks as if it's set in for the day,' Kay remarked. 'I'll drive for you, if you like, Nurse.'

'Thank you, perhaps you would. But you see how open the roads are between the villages. If these conditions prevail much longer, we're going to have to wait for the snow plough to clear the way for us.'

Kay found it difficult when she started driving. The snow collected on the windscreen much faster than the wipers could dispose of it, and the car felt unsteady under her hands.

Nevertheless, they went on slowly, and eventually reached the next village. Kay heaved a long sigh when she saw the first houses, and Nurse Harmon smiled.

'It does make the day more interesting,' she said as they left the car. 'But you have to have a special kind of temperament for this work.'

'And a great deal of determination, I should think,' Kay added.

There followed the same routine, which they had followed in Cairnburn, and Kay met more patients. She was relieved to find that the work itself would give her no worries, her only fears were that the weather might hold her up, especially when she had to turn out for some emergency.

When they left Brechnockie to go on to Kilbernian, the weather was much worse, and Kay estimated that three inches of snow had fallen since they had set out that morning. They had seven miles to drive between the two villages, and their progress was very slow. Kay did the driving, and they were reduced to a crawl on the narrow roads which twisted and turned across the moors.

'Shall we get back to town after this last visit?' Kay demanded worriedly, and Nurse Harmon smiled.

'Don't worry! I expect we'll get back. If we don't we'll get help from the villagers. That's one of the blessings of this job: everyone pitches in to help, no matter what the trouble may be.'

Kay nodded and they went on. But Kay was worried, for the worst of the winter was yet to come, and she knew it. When they eventually reached Kilbernian she was very relieved, and they left the car and walked their round. They had seven calls altogether, and two of those were young wives who were expecting babies. Kay could expect to be called out at any time after she had taken over on Sunday, and she found herself praying that the weather would not be so bad as to stop her or add complications to her new job.

'Well,' Nurse Harmon said at length, when they had left the house of the last patient, 'that's the end of the regular round for the day. We've done quite well, considering the weather.'

'We can go back to town now?' Kay demanded.

'Yes. I've taken you around all the places you will cover. If we can make good time back to town, we'll have a quick lunch and then take the Clinic.'

'You're kept very busy each day, then,' Kay said. They had returned to the car, and Kay began the difficult job of driving back to Stranduthie.

'Oh, yes! This afternoon I help at the Clinic in Stranduthie. Tomorrow I hold a Clinic in Kilbernian, so I arrange my normal rounds accordingly. No sense in making two trips to the village in one day. I hold village Clinics every other day, starting with Cairnburn on Mondays, Brechnockie on Wednesdays and Kilbernian on Fridays. Tuesday and Thursday afternoons are spent in town.'

'And your day off?' Kay queried.

'There is a relief system in operation. All the duties are covered, don't you worry.'

Kay nodded, and concentrated upon her driving. It was fortunate that they did not meet many vehicles on the road, for she found it difficult to keep the car on a straight course along the twisting road. Eventually, however, they reached town, and she sighed heavily in relief when they came to her uncle's house.

Kay glanced at her watch. 'It's almost one-thirty now, Nurse. I'll attend the Clinic with you this afternoon. What time do you usually get there?'

'By two-thirty. I'll come and pick you up.'

'There's no need to. I can catch a bus. It will drop me fairly close to the Clinic. I'll see you there in about an hour, shall I?'

'Very well. I'm glad to see that you're still keen, despite the hard morning we've had.' Nurse Harmon smiled, and her eyes were bright.

'I must learn all my duties before you finish, Nurse,' Kay said, as she alighted from the car. She paused before slamming the door. 'I'll see you this afternoon at about two-thirty, then.'

'Good-bye,' Nurse Harmon said, settling herself at the wheel, and Kay shut the door and stepped back to watch the determined old lady drive slowly away.

Aunt Margaret was waiting impatiently for Kay, and had her lunch ready. They sat together in the big kitchen and Kay gave her aunt an account of her morning's activities. She was enthusiastic about her new job, and her eagerness pleased the older woman.

'You don't think it is going to be too much for you, do you?' Aunt Margaret demanded.

'Certainly not! If Nurse Harmon can cope, then so can I!'

'That's true, but Nurse Harmon has been doing that job for as long as I can remember.'

'She had to start some time, and so have I.'

'What are you going to do this afternoon?'

'I'll go to the Clinic.' Kay pushed aside her plate. 'That was good, Aunt. I really enjoyed it, and I was ready for it.'

'Good. Now why don't you go and sit in the arm-chair for a bit before rushing off to the Clinic. I'll make sure you leave in good time.'

Kay smiled her thanks and did as her aunt had suggested. When she left for the Clinic, half an hour later, she felt a new woman.

Just as in the morning, Kay learnt a great deal during the course of the afternoon. She met several members of the Clinic staff, and soon discovered what would be expected of her every week. When it was time to leave, she drove home with Nurse Harmon and they planned the following day's itinerary.

Although she had merely accompanied Nurse Harmon that day, Kay found that she was unusually tired when she reached home. She paused for a moment in the hall and took off her fur-lined boots, thrusting her feet into her slippers. Aunt Margaret appeared, smiling with pleasure at the sight of her, and Kay realized how pleased she was to be home.

'You look tired,' Aunt Margaret said.

'I feel it. I don't know what it will be like when I'm doing the work on my own. My main worry is that I shan't be able to reach my patients — and that's quite likely if the weather gets any worse. Are there any times, Aunt, when Uncle can't get through to his patients? He covers the same area as myself.'

'There are times,' the older woman replied, with a serious face. 'I've known him take three hours to do a trip that would normally only take thirty minutes, and sometimes he's been unable to get through at all until the snow ploughs have been out.'

'No wonder he looks as if he's done more than his share.' Kay could not keep her mind from that other source of worry: her uncle's health. 'Have you spoken to him yet about cutting down on his work?'

'No.' Her aunt shook her head slowly. 'I shall have to find the right approach.'

'Get him to take another partner into the practice,' Kay said. 'That would be the easiest way out of it.'

'And that's easier said than done!' Aunt Margaret shook her head.

★ ★ ★

When Clive appeared about seven that evening, having finished surgery, Kay inquired of him her uncle's whereabouts, and learned that Edgar Duncan had gone to Kilbernian to answer an emergency call.

'I wanted to go in his place, but he wouldn't hear of it,' Clive said, his dark eyes showing concern. 'He gets more difficult day by day, as if he knows that he's doing too much but resents my trying to take some of his duties off his shoulders. He's so independent that one just can't help him.'

'I'll have a talk with him when he does come home,' Kay said.

'Be careful what you say to him because he's touchy, and you could do more harm than good by trying to help.'

'That's more or less what Aunt Margaret said, but we couldn't make it any worse for him, could we? The least we could do is persuade him to take more care of himself.'

'Try it, but be cautious in your approach.' He studied her face for a moment. They were in the front sitting-room, she at one side of the fire with an unread magazine in her hands and he at the other side, reading the newspaper. His feet were thrust into slippers, and he seemed thoroughly at home as he relaxed after his hard, cold day.

Clive returned his attention to his newspaper, but not for long. He looked up again a few moments later.

'Kay?'

'Yes?'

'Have you decided yet which day of the week you will have off?'

'No. I don't suppose it matters very much. One day is much the same as another around here, I suppose.'

'Take Fridays off,' he suggested.

'Why Fridays in particular?'

'Because I have Fridays off, and we could get together if we are off duty at the same time.'

She smiled and nodded without hesitation. 'Friday it will be. I'll let the Department know about it first thing in the morning. But what is there to do around here on a day off?'

'Are you any good at winter sports?' His dark eyes were gleaming as he regarded her.

'I can skate and ski,' she retorted. 'When I was in London, I used to take winter holidays in Switzerland.'

'Well that's good news. I ski quite a lot, but it's no fun to go out alone. You'll have to get some skis and then we'll have some sport'

'That's the best suggestion I've heard since I've been here,' Kay said, smiling. 'It makes me even more glad that I decided to leave London and come to Stranduthie.'

'Ah! But I doubt that you are as glad as I am, Kay,' said Clive, his eyes twinkling.

'Why do you say that?' She was intrigued.

'Well, if you hadn't come, I might never have met you,' he said lightly.

With a rosy tinge colouring her cheeks, Kay bent her head and pretended to read her magazine . . .

It wasn't until much later that Edgar Duncan put in an appearance; when she heard him in the hall, Kay got up and went to open the door to look at her uncle. She saw that he was looking pale, tired and very cold, but he smiled as he glanced at her.

'Hello, Kay. You look warm as toast. Do me a favour, will you?'

'Certainly.' She went out to him,

taking his coat from his cold hands and putting it into the cloakroom.

'Pour me a generous glass of whisky, please.'

She nodded and hurried to obey and, when she returned to him, he was sitting on the chair in the hall and putting on his slippers. He thanked her and took the glass from her hands, gulping at the liquor; then he smiled and nodded as he looked up at her.

'I needed that,' he said.

'You've had a long day, Uncle.' She took the glass from him while he finished putting on his slippers, and then he stood up, reaching for the glass again, and she watched him take another gulp of whisky.

'That's the way it is for a doctor,' he commented, putting an arm around her shoulder. 'But how about your day? I saw Nurse Harmon this evening and she said how pleased she was that you are taking over from her. You're very dedicated to your work, she informs me, and it was good news, Kay. I hope you will make out all right.'

'There's no need to worry about me — but what about you?' she demanded. He looked into her eyes for a moment, and she saw a shadow cross his face.

'I'm all right. I've been doing these rounds for more years than I care to remember. I could do my work blindfold, I do believe.'

'But that isn't the point, Uncle,' she said smoothly, and in low tones. 'You're not really very well, are you?'

He stared at her for a moment, then glanced around the hall as if fearful that she had been overheard. 'Come with me into the study,' he said.

Kay nodded and followed him along the hall to the study. He closed the door after her and then motioned for her to take a seat, while he moved round behind his desk. His face seemed even paler as he sat down.

'Kay, you're keen sighted if you can see there's something wrong with me,' he said.

'Not keen sighted at all, Uncle,' she

retorted. 'Clive told me that you should cut down on your duties.'

He sighed heavily, but shook his head. 'I'm all right, I tell you.'

'You can't fool me, Uncle. If you can pull the wool over Aunt Margaret's eyes, you can't kid me. What are you trying to do? What about Aunt Margaret, if you kill yourself with too much work?'

He shrugged and shook his head. 'What can I do?' he demanded. 'I can't sit back while there's all this work to do. I can't push it all on Clive, can I?'

'Have you thought about bringing in a third partner, and cutting down on your share?' she asked sharply.

'It has passed through my mind. The practice has grown a great deal in the past years.'

'Well, why haven't you taken steps, Uncle? If you were a patient instead of a doctor, you would want your doctor to do the best he could for you, wouldn't you?'

'That's obviously true.' He smiled

faintly. 'All right, Kay. I'll think over what you've said.'

'That's not good enough,' she insisted. 'If you have a heart condition, Uncle, then you've got to do something about it now. Don't leave it too late. You haven't all that much time to spare — but I think you know that, don't you?'

'I suppose I do! It's become increasingly obvious to me over the past week, and I suppose it will become even more pressing as the winter goes on. I need a rest, and a long one, Kay. I tell you what, I'll bring in a locum and take some time off. I hate admitting it but, for the moment, I think I've had enough.'

Kay smiled at him. 'Well, now you've admitted it to yourself, perhaps you'll do something. I won't say anything to Aunt, but you could broach the subject to her this evening and set her mind at rest.'

Edgar stood up. 'I'll do that, Kay, and thank you, my dear, for putting this matter into perspective for me. I'm so pleased you've come here to live. We all need you, you know.'

Kay went back to the sitting-room, her heart filled to overflowing with emotion. Clive looked up at her entrance, then got to his feet. He stood before the open fire while she crossed to his side.

'How is he?' he demanded.

'Worn out.' She sighed as she turned her back to the fire, and their shoulders touched. 'But I've had a word with him and he's going to bring in a locum to take his place while he has a rest.'

'Good!' Clive looked down into her eyes. 'How did you manage to get him to agree to that?'

'I appealed to his common sense,' she said slowly. 'But I think he's feeling so badly now that he knows he's got to do something, and my intervention was all he needed to bring matters to a head.'

'Good for you! So we'll get something done, after all. You certainly must be a very persuasive girl, Kay. I can see your patients won't stand a chance with you to nurse them!' he teased.

Kay laughed, but went on more seriously: 'Will you be able to cope with the rounds, Clive, until the locum arrives?'

'Oh, yes. Don't worry about that. I'll persuade your uncle to do surgery twice a day, which will leave me free to struggle through the snow on the visits.' He gave her a boyish grin as he finished: 'I think you should have come here a few months ago, Kay.'

'Why? You don't think it's too late now to help him, do you?' Kay was suddenly worried.

'No.' He shook his head. 'But it would have made things a lot easier for your aunt.' He smiled as he watched her face. 'And I would have known you sooner.'

She smiled, her eyes on his face. 'That's a rather significant statement to make, isn't it?' she murmured.

'It is, and I'm a little surprised by it myself. But I can't wait to get to know you better, Kay. I wish the winter was gone. This part of the country is very beautiful in the spring, and there's a lot more scope for doing things.'

'It will come,' she said softly, and felt strangely impatient herself. The idea of getting to know Clive better was more attractive than she would admit, even to herself . . .

*   *   *

The next two days seemed to Kay to pass quickly. She went out with Nurse Harmon during the days in order to familiarize herself with the routines which she would have to follow when she took over her duties; and she found that, true to her fears, the worst enemy she would have as a district nurse was the weather. But the roads were not yet impassable, and the little car which they used seemed to be able to get through without too much trouble.

On Saturday afternoon, Clive took Kay ski-ing on the local slopes. She had borrowed skis from a neighbour and, whether it was the fact that she was enjoying the pastime or Clive's company, her eyes shone and she was filled with excitement as the afternoon progressed.

Clive proved to be a perfect skier, and she found it difficult to keep up with him. When they stopped on a high slope overlooking the town, Clive complimented her upon her skill, and she flushed with pleasure.

'I need a lot more experience,' she said. 'I've learned the fundamentals, but one can hardly get enough experience in England.'

'You should be able to get all the experience you need around here and during this winter,' he retorted. They were watching a dozen or so assorted skiers darting hither and thither across the hillside.

'There'll be a lot more snow to come before we see spring,' Kay remarked. She was thoughtful for a moment while she studied their surroundings. There had been a heavy frost the night before and, where snow had fallen from the bushes and branches, there were delicate patterns of frost in the hard ice. The air was very keen and sharp, and Kay's breath was steaming with each exhalation.

'We'll get more than our share, don't you worry,' Clive retorted with a smile.

'But I am worried.' Kay shook her head. 'Although I'm enjoying this afternoon very much, I would rather not see the snow at all.'

'You're still worried about getting through to your patients, aren't you?' he demanded.

'Of course! Surely that thought is ever present in your mind at this time of the year.'

'It is, but I don't worry about it!' He placed a hand upon her shoulder. 'I'll always help you, should you ever run into difficulties. There's nothing to worry about. The first thing the local council does, when there's been a heavy snow-fall, is to send the snow ploughs out to open up the roads; but if you're so worried about getting through, then just stop to consider. The very means of making it are in your possession right now.'

'What do you mean?' She stared at him with narrowed eyes, and he chuckled.

'Has anyone ever told you how beautiful you are?' he demanded.

'Don't change the subject,' she said sharply. 'What do you mean?'

'How do you suppose people in countries which get far more snow than we do make out when the usual forms of transport can't be used?'

'They use, sledges.'

'Or skis!' He smiled, shaking his head. 'You can ski. So what's to prevent you putting your medical supplies in some sort of a haversack and using skis to get around the villages?'

Kay couldn't tell if he were joking or not, but she fancied he was suggesting a sound idea, and she frowned as she considered it.

'On the face of it, I think it is a good suggestion,' she said at length.

'Of course it is! When I was in Switzerland, the doctor I was staying with used skis all the year round when he had to visit patients living very high in the Alps. They're the perfect form of transport.'

Kay nodded, her mind suddenly relieved of the worry which had nagged her constantly since her arrival. She could ski well enough to make use of that mode of travelling! So there was no problem.

'I can see that you like the idea,' Clive said. 'I was only joking in the first instance, but it is a practical suggestion all the same. If I couldn't get through by car, then I'd certainly strap on skis and make it that way.'

Kay smiled her thanks for the suggestion and, before she knew what was happening, found herself being drawn towards him. Clive had dropped his skis, which he had been holding since he had taken them off, and had put both his arms round Kay. As her skis joined his on the snow, she gave herself up to his kiss with a sigh of happiness.

'Kay, I'm beginning to fall in love with you,' Clive said huskily, when they drew apart.

'In so short a time?' she whispered.

'Why not? I took a liking to you the instant we met, and I haven't been trying to fight my feelings.' He looked down into her face as he pulled her back into his embrace. 'There's something about you, Kay, that knocks the bottom out of all my resolutions to stay away from romance.'

'Really?' She had to fight the lump in her throat in order to speak. 'Why should you want to remain aloof, Clive?'

'No particular reason, except that I think a doctor should devote all his energies to his work. But that was before I met you. Now, my work doesn't seem to be so important any more!'

Before Kay could say anything in reply, Clive's lips sought hers again, and this time the kiss was long and passionate. Silence pressed in about them, holding them together in an isolation that seemed unreal. But his mouth against hers was real enough, and so were the emotions building up inside her. When he released her, Kay was breathless, and she bent to put on her skis with her mind a riot of conflicting thoughts.

When she straightened, Clive took her arm. She looked steadily into his eyes, telling herself that he attracted her greatly, that she could fall in love with him so easily. They had been thrown together by Fate. The fact that they lived in the same house and saw each other every day had outwitted time; she knew as much about him in these circumstances as it would have taken an ordinary girl at least a month to find out. But she had always been convinced that time did not matter in love.

'We'd better start back to where we

left the car,' he said in unsteady tones. 'I'm taking the evening surgery, and duty beckons. But before we go, Kay, I want to talk rather seriously to you. I think I caught you rather off your guard, but I don't want you to think that my attitude towards you is merely flirtations. I've never been that kind of man. I have come to care a great deal about you in the week we've known each other. Of course, I had heard about you from your aunt, which prepared my mind for meeting you, and I knew even before you arrived that you were the kind of girl I could love. If that sounds strange to you, then I apologize, but that's the kind of receptive mood you found me in when you came.'

'You'll have to give me time to collect myself,' she said in quivering tones. 'I don't know what you've done to me, but you're having quite an effect upon me.'

'Take all the time in the world,' he said boldly. 'I have a feeling that everything is going to work out right.'

He grinned, his eyes sparkling. 'Now I'll race you down the slopes to the car.'

Kay pushed off and sped down the slope, her eyes narrowed against the wind; but a few moments later, having put on his own skis, Clive passed her, turning to grin and wave. He gradually drew ahead, and Kay shook her head as she slowed a little. She watched him going on, and her thoughts were dreamy.

What had Clive done to her? How could he attract her so? A week ago, she had not known he existed, and now she could not get him out of her mind. She shook her head in bewilderment.

When she reached the car, he had already taken off his skis and was standing at the side of the vehicle awaiting her arrival. She took off her skis and he put them into the boot for her. Kay was still breathless when he helped her into the car.

'Will you take me to Nurse Harmon's home?' she asked, as he drove slowly along the narrow road to town. 'She's almost finished her duties now, and I'll pick up the car from her and take over. I shall be answering all calls for the nurse as from this evening.'

'Well, let's pray you'll be lucky enough not to have any calls tonight! And of course I'll take you to Nurse Harmon's, though I'm afraid I shan't be able to come in because of getting back in time for surgery.'

When he dropped her off outside Nurse Harmon's home, Kay paused to look into his face, and he waited, despite the fact that he had so little time left. She nodded slowly, and a smile curved his mouth.

'Do you like what you see?' he demanded.

'Yes.' She nodded emphatically. 'I'll see you later, Clive. Don't delay now, because your time is running out.'

He smiled, and she closed the door and stepped back, waiting for him to drive away before turning to go to Nurse Harmon's cottage.

'Hello, Kay, do come in,' Nurse Harmon greeted, when she opened the door.

'I thought I'd come and take over from you now, to save your turning out on your last evening,' Kay said, as she crossed the threshold.

'That's very kind of you!' Nurse Harmon's eyes were bright with emotion. 'I've just got in from a confinement, and I'm expecting to be called out again later tonight. I'll carry on, if you wish, until tomorrow morning.'

'No, I'll take over and get ready to plunge into my duties,' Kay said. 'I do hope you're going to enjoy your retirement. I expect you'll find it difficult to adjust after so many years of listening for the telephone to ring and hurrying out at all times of the day or night.'

'I shall be very sorry to give up, of course — but, frankly, my dear, I think age has beaten me at last. I doubt that I could have gone on much longer. Now, what about a cup of tea?'

'That sounds lovely,' said Kay brightly. 'Can I give you a hand?'

'No. You just take off your anorak, and find a seat. I shan't be a moment.'

Over tea, the older woman gave Kay the full list of patients and added some more advice to that which she had already given. Finally, she gave Kay the keys to the car and, with a slight tremor in her voice, wished the young girl good luck. As Kay left the cottage and climbed into the car, she realized that there were tears in her own eyes.

She felt rather depressed when she reached home, and had to force herself to smile before she went inside. Aunt Margaret greeted her, and Kay learned that the locum, who had been expected that afternoon to see about taking over from Edgar Duncan, had arrived and been found suitable.

'He's a very bold young man,' Aunt Margaret said, 'but he seems most suitable and very able. He's in the study with your uncle now.'

'What's his name?' Kay asked.

'Frank Munro. He's from Glasgow. He's coming to stay here with us for three months in the first instance.'

'That's wonderful!' Kay felt cheerfulness flood into her. 'If Uncle Edgar rests for three months, it will make a new man of him.'

. . . Kay met Frank Munro some time later, when they all sat down to a light meal, to which the young doctor had also been invited before he caught his train back to Glasgow. Clive had not yet finished in surgery so he wasn't present.

Frank Munro was tall and slim, with dark hair and brown eyes. He came forward readily with outstretched hand when Kay was introduced to him, and he held her hand far longer than was necessary.

'I'm very pleased to meet you,' he said in cultured tones. 'It's going to be a pleasure working here, I can assure you. Take as long as you need to get well, Doctor.' He glanced at Edgar Duncan as he spoke.

'Kay has just taken over as the

district nurse,' Edgar replied. 'She's only been here a week. She's been working in London until now.'

'Let's sit down at the table before the meal gets cold,' Aunt Margaret said.

Munro held Kay's chair for her, and she felt confused as she thanked him. He smiled knowingly and went to sit down opposite; and he monopolized the conversation, asking a great many pointed questions, both about his future work with them and about Kay's previous life.

'Have you met Dr. Farrell?' Kay asked, when she found herself rather hard pressed by his questions.

'Yes. As a matter of fact, I knew Farrell when we were students. I must say I'm surprised to find him here in such an out-of-the-way spot — great things were promised for him when he was a student. He was expected to go right to the top, and take all the short cuts on the way.'

'Really!' Edgar Duncan was instantly interested. 'What could have happened then, do you suppose, to send him to me?'

'That doesn't matter,' Kay said, before she realized what was in her mind. 'He's an able doctor, and has worked here efficiently, hasn't he?'

'He has most certainly,' Edgar responded. 'Was there some sort of a tragedy in his life then, Munro?'

'There was talk of a woman,' came the unexpected reply, and Frank Munro looked boldly into Kay's face as he spoke. 'You have to watch your step where Clive Farrell is concerned. He had the reputation of being a real Casanova!'

'Well, that's very interesting,' Kay forced herself to say, and she laughed lightly, although a cold hand seemed to touch her spine. She had the feeling then that she and Frank Munro would not get along at all well; she didn't like his easy smile nor the way he monopolized the conversation. There had been a note suspiciously like envy in his tones when he had talked of

Clive, and she fancied that Clive was a far better man in every respect, despite what Munro had said about him.

However, she had no intention of being drawn into any conversation that might feature Clive, in his absence, and as soon as the meal was over she excused herself on the grounds that she had to prepare for any emergency; and she went up to her room in a deeply thoughtful frame of mind . . .

3

There was no emergency call for Kay that night, although she slept fitfully in anticipation. When she awoke next morning, she leapt out of bed and hurried to the window, twitching the curtain aside to peer out at the gloomy day. Her heart sank when she saw that there had been a heavy fall of snow during the night, and she stared out silently, fascinated by the brilliant mantle which had covered over all the dirty tracks and levelled out the drifts.

Her first thought was for the car, which had been left out because there was no room in the garage for it. She knew she would be called out at some time during the day, although it was a Sunday, because one expectant mother at least was now overdue.

Kay hurriedly dressed and went down. She found her aunt, an inveterate early riser, in the kitchen, and she paused just long enough to have a cup of tea before donning a coat and hurrying outside to ensure that the car would start. The engine started easily, much to Kay's relief, but when she decided to have a run around the block to check the condition of the road, she found the utmost difficulty in driving without skidding. The car was very unsteady, and only the slightest extra acceleration was sufficient to make the rear end of the vehicle veer to one side or the other.

When she went back into the house she told her aunt of the situation, and went to check through the notes which Nurse Harmon had given her regarding the patients on the current list. She could certainly expect to be called out to attend a confinement during the day, and she was naturally worried by the road conditions.

She had only just finished her breakfast when the telephone rang, and her heart seemed to miss a beat as she hurried from the kitchen in answer.

'Your first case?' Aunt Margaret demanded at her back, and Kay shook her head.

'It might be for the doctor,' she said, 'but I am expecting a call.' She lifted the receiver and gave her name, and there was an immediate reply from a harassed sounding man.

'Nurse, this is Stuart Lachlan. It's my wife — she'd like you to come immediately. The baby is on the way.'

'All right, Mr. Lachlan. Has she described her pains?'

'They're coming every thirty minutes or so, Nurse. She started about an hour ago.'

'Very well. I'll be in to see you within the hour.'

'The roads are pretty bad today, Nurse.'

'It will be all right. There's nothing to worry about. I'll be there as soon as possible.'

The line went dead, and Kay took a deep breath. She hung up and turned to find Aunt Margaret standing at her elbow. She nodded in answer to the unspoken question in her aunt's eyes.

'It's Mrs. Lachlan over at Brechnockie — she'll be having her baby today, probably this afternoon. Clive is her doctor. Is he about yet, do you know?'

'I heard him moving around upstairs a short time ago.'

'I'd better inform him of the situation, then be on my way,' Kay said. 'It's her first baby, and she was very nervous when I saw her the other day with Nurse Harmon.'

Aunt Margaret nodded her understanding. 'Be very careful on the roads,' she warned. 'There was a lot of snow last night and, being Sunday, the snow plough might not be out so early.'

'I'll get through,' Kay said firmly, and went on up the stairs to see Clive. She tapped at his door and he came immediately in answer, dressed in casual trousers and a thick white sweater.

'Good morning, Kay,' he said, smiling. 'You're up early for a Sunday.'

'I've just had a call about Mrs. Lachlan, and I'm on my way to visit her immediately. You're her doctor, Clive. Will you be going in to see her?'

'The doctor usually calls after the event,' he said with a smile. 'But I'll go along with you now, if you wish. What are the roads like?'

'Bad this morning. There's been a lot more snow during the night. But, don't worry, I'll be all right. Let me go alone, and I'll call you after I've examined Mrs. Lachlan to let you know how she is.'

'All right.' He nodded wisely. 'This is your first case, isn't it? I hope it goes off all right, Kay.'

'So do I,' she replied. 'Good-bye now. I don't know when I shall get back. If she's well advanced I shan't bother to return; I have one or two other calls to make in the village, and I'll do them while awaiting the happy event.'

'Don't forget to let me know the

situation,' he said, and took hold of her hands. 'Good luck, and drive carefully.' He pulled her into his arms and kissed her lightly, and Kay forgot her anxieties for a moment in the pleasure of his nearness. Then she pulled herself away.

'See you later,' she said lightly, and departed. She found Aunt Margaret in the hall, and asked the older woman to take any messages which might come through in her absence. 'I'll check with you after I've seen Mrs. Lachlan,' she said. 'Good-bye now, Aunt. I don't know when I'll be back.'

She left the house and paused before getting into the car to check the equipment in the boot. Satisfied that she had everything necessary for the case, she slid behind the wheel and slammed the door. Then she started the car and began to drive to Brechnockie. A snow plough had been along the main streets in the town, and Kay sighed her relief as she made good speed to the town limits but, when she reached the first stretch of winding country road, she found the snow was inches thick, and there were very few car tracks through it. She realized that it was going to take her a considerable time to reach the village.

She passed through Cairnburn and took the road which led to Brechnockie. Now she found it even more difficult to make progress because the road was like a switchback, and traffic which had used the route before her had made the inclines slippery, causing Kay's heart to flutter nervously each time she found the car hesitating on the upper stretches of each hill. She dropped down in gear and crawled on, and eventually she came into Brechnockie.

Her relief at her arrival was echoed by the man who opened the door of the Lachlan household to her.

'Thank heavens you're here, Nurse,' he gasped, a tall, powerful man in his middle twenties. 'I've been worried about the wife. The pains are getting worse. I'll take you up to her.'

Kay followed him up the stairs. She found Mrs. Lachlan tense and nervous, and thoroughly relieved to see her. Kay greeted the young woman lightly, intending to put her at ease.

'I thought perhaps you wouldn't be able to get through the snow drifts, Nurse,' Mrs. Lachlan said.

'It was a bit tricky in places, but I'm here, so the worst of it is over.' Kay looked around the warm room, and smiled when she saw a cot set up by the large bed. Baby clothes were laid out on the cot cover, and when she went closer she saw a hot-water bottle in the cot.

'We're all ready,' the woman said with a nervous smile. 'I don't think I'm going to be long over this, Nurse.'

'It's difficult to judge with the first one,' Kay said. 'Relax now and I'll examine you.'

'Well?' Mrs. Lachlan demanded after the examination.

'Everything is normal, and it's just a matter of waiting,' Kay replied. 'I would say this afternoon.'

'Will you be going now?' the woman demanded.

'I have some calls to make in the village, and I'll attend to them, then come back and see how you're doing. I shan't go back to town, just in case.' Kay opened her bag and prepared an injection. 'I'll give you this to help matters, then I'll inform the doctor. I'll be back in about an hour, and we should know a bit more about the situation by then.'

'Thank you, Nurse.' The woman was more relaxed now.

Kay walked to the door. 'You don't have to lie down on the bed all the time, Mrs. Lachlan. Move around the room, and you'll find it will help if you try to do things. But keep a check on the times of your pains, won't you?'

'Yes, Nurse.'

'See you in about an hour, then,' Kay responded, and left the room. She went down the stairs and Mr. Lachlan opened the inner door. 'It won't be quite yet,' Kay told him. 'Some time in the afternoon, I expect.'

'Oh!' He was both relieved and disappointed.

Kay told him her intentions, and he nodded. He opened the door for her, and Kay departed, promising to return shortly. She left her car and walked along the street, making the other calls that were scheduled. Then she telephoned Clive from the public call box.

'Hello, Kay,' he said. 'I've been worrying about you. Did you get through without too much trouble?'

'It was a bit difficult in places, but if it's never any worse than this morning, then I shan't grumble about it.'

'The weather forecast is that there's a lot more snow on the way,' he told her.

'Well, you needn't sound so pleased about it,' she retorted lightly.

'Why not? We can always go ski-ing, can't we? I thoroughly enjoyed yesterday afternoon and I can't wait to go again! However, to get back to business.

What about your confinement case?'

'Some time this afternoon,' Kay prophesied.

'Will you be coming home to lunch?'

'I don't know. I shall go and check with Mrs. Lachlan again when I've finished my normal round, and if the indications are still the same, then I'll go on to Kilbernian and make my calls there. I'll come home then, and do the calls in Cairnburn this afternoon on my way back here.'

'You seem to have it all logically worked out!' Clive chuckled.

Kay laughed lightly. 'Has there been any inquiry for me?' she asked. 'Aunt Margaret said she would take any messages that might come in.'

'Just a moment and I'll check.' There was silence for a few minutes, then Clive came back to report that there had been no calls for her.

'Thank you,' she said. 'I'll get the rest of the calls done here, Clive, then check with Mrs. Lachlan again. Then I'll go on to Kilbernian. I'll ring again if I have to make any changes but, all being well, I should be home by one.'

'I'll be looking for you. Be careful on the roads, Kay.'

'I will.' She smiled as she replaced the receiver. She left the box and the cold air struck at her, stinging her face. She glanced up at the overcast sky, then tightened her grip upon her bag and walked on along the road.

When she went back to the Lachlan house, she found the situation unchanged, and confirmed her opinion that the baby would be born during the late afternoon or early evening. She told Mr. Lachlan of her plans, and informed him that he was to ring her aunt's house should there be any significant change in his wife's condition. He nodded apprehensively, and she tried to reassure him as she departed.

'I'll be back here at about two-thirty,' she promised. 'There won't be anything doing before then.'

Driving on to Kilbernian, Kay stopped at the village and made her calls. There were two expectant mothers she had to visit here, but neither of them was due to give birth for a week or more. In a short time she was ready to continue homewards, and paused at the telephone box in the village to check with her aunt if there had been any more calls for her. She learned that there was nothing to report, and decided to go home, highly satisfied with her morning's activities.

Aunt Margaret had lunch ready by the time Kay had returned, and Edgar Duncan poured her a sherry as they awaited the meal. Clive put in an appearance, and Kay described her morning. She was light-hearted now, because the first morning was behind her. The fact that the snow-fall hadn't delayed her much had worked wonders with her morale, and she felt as if all her problems had faded.

After lunch she sat in the large sitting-room with Clive for half an hour, but she could not relax. She wanted to get into the village of

Cairnburn and attend to her calls there before going on to the confinement at Brechnockie. When she showed her restlessness, Clive smiled.

'Give me a call from Brechnockie when the child is about due, Kay, and I'll drive out,' he told her. 'Everything is normal, as far as you can tell, isn't it?'

'Yes. I don't anticipate any trouble. But I'll keep in touch with you.'

'Good,' he said. 'Now, promise me you'll be careful driving back there.'

'I promise,' she answered demurely.

Clive got to his feet and came across to her, kissing her lightly, and Kay looked into his eyes before she turned away. She saw tenderness in his expression, and her pulses quickened as emotion welled within her. The future promised to be marvellous, she told herself.

'See you later,' she said, and departed. . . . After making her calls in Cairnburn, Kay drove on to Brechnockie and, when she drew in at the kerb outside the Lachlan house, she paused for a moment to stare through the windscreen. A few flakes of snow were beginning to fall again, and the sky seemed laden with bulging clouds all anxious to shed their loads — but it didn't matter to her now. As she got out of the car, Mr. Lachlan emerged from the house and hurried to take her case from her, and they went into the house together.

'How is Mrs. Lachlan now?' Kay demanded.

'Still all right, although the pains are worse and coming very much quicker,' was the prompt reply. 'I have been getting rather anxious, Nurse, but it's all right now you're here.'

Kay smiled at his words. She felt touched by the knowledge that she was needed here; and the fact that people had faith in her skill made all the years of training seem even more worth-while. They went up to the bedroom, and an examination of her patient informed Kay that the birth would not be long delayed . . .

The confinement proceeded without complications, and at four-twenty in the afternoon a boy was born. Kay was as excited as her patient, and when mother and child were presentable, she called in the waiting father. It was touching to see the man with his wife, and there was a deep feeling of humility within Kay as she went downstairs. She had a cup of tea, and was almost ready to go when Clive arrived. He went up to see the mother, and a few minutes later he was ready to leave.

'I'll be in tomorrow morning,' Kay told her patient.

'Thank you, Nurse, for everything,' Mrs. Lachlan whispered.

Clive was waiting outside in his car when Kay came out. She put her bag into her own car, then going to Clive's car, she got in at his side for a few moments.

'Tired?' he asked.

'A little. It seems to have been a long day.'

'It will be a memorable one from your point of view,' Clive said wisely. 'I doubt if you'll ever forget it. Your first confinement is behind you.' He took hold of her hands. 'You look tired. It's been quite a strain on you. Have you finished for the day now?'

'I think so. There are no more confinements due for a week at least.'

'Then let's start homewards, shall we? Let's sit in front of the fire in the sitting-room and forget about this cold, grey world outside.'

'You're on call, aren't you?' she asked.

'Yes. But I think we'll be lucky this evening. There'll be no one in this area needing the services of a doctor tonight.'

'When does Dr. Munro start with you?'

'Tomorrow morning. He'll be arriving some time this evening!' There was a trace of something like dismay in Clive's tones.

'You knew him as a student, didn't you?'

'Yes. I didn't like him very much, but he's a good doctor, I believe.'

'I think I took a dislike to him as soon as I saw him,' Kay said slowly. 'I don't know why I should! But he was just a little bit too friendly. I may be wrong, but I don't like that type. Of course, he may have been trying to make a good impression because he was coming to work with you, but I'll reserve judgement on him until I get to know him better.'

Clive smiled. 'I'm glad to hear that you didn't take an instant liking to him,' he said. 'Most girls did, I seem to remember. He was a ladies' man, if ever there was one, and we all thought he would fail to qualify because he spent so little time on his studies.'

'He said you were little short of brilliant when you were a student,' Kay said slowly.

'Did he?' Clive sounded surprised. 'I must say, I thought he was always a little bit envious of me.'

'Well, no matter what he was like as a student, he's coming to relieve Uncle, and that's all that matters,' Kay said. 'Look, I don't know why we're sitting here in the cold, do you? I'll follow you home, shall I?'

'All right.' He leaned sideways and kissed her gently, and Kay clutched at him, beset by sudden, powerful emotions. She kissed him hard in return, and saw surprise come into his face. 'Your feelings seem to be as deep as mine,' he whispered, and she nodded silently.

'They seem to be. Is it a good sign, would you say?'

'I think it is! But it's up to you to make your own decision on that.'

Kay smiled and got out of the car, slamming the door and hurrying to her own vehicle. When Clive drove away, she followed him at a distance, her thoughts in a fever of happy anticipation . . .

* * *

That first Sunday on duty set the pattern of Kay's life afterwards. Her days were busy, and she was always aware of a sense of urgency surrounding her. She set out in her car before daylight, and didn't finish until well after darkness had fallen at the end of each short day.

In one way, it was a blessing that she was very busy that first week, because Frank Munro arrived on the Sunday that she commenced her duties, and he quickly settled into the household. The trouble was that he tried from the very outset to attract her, and made himself something of a nuisance whenever he caught her alone in the house. He kept putting a hand upon her shoulder, or talked very significantly about taking her out, flattering her outrageously, even when she told him that she was attracted to Clive. When he started talking disparagingly about Clive, however, she silenced him angrily and refused to listen despite his persistence.

That first week was understandably

very tense for Kay, and she was not sorry when Friday came and she was off duty for the day. Clive had the same day off, and they arranged to go for a drive. A slight thaw had set in during the week and the roads were comparatively free of snow; but weather forecasts indicated that a great deal more snow was on the way. Determined not to let that news worry her on her day off, Kay leaned back in her seat and relaxed.

'Where are we going, Clive?' she asked.

'I'm taking you into Inverglen. We'll have lunch at the hotel there, and this afternoon we'll go over the castle.' He glanced at her. 'I hope you like looking over old places — I spend a lot of my time doing that. I go to the castle every month or so; it's not in ruins, and they have a wonderful museum there.'

'Lovely,' Kay declared. 'It's just the sort of thing I like doing, and today is perfect for a trip back into history. But are you a romantic, Clive?'

'I suppose, as a doctor, I ought to answer no to that,' he retorted. 'In previous centuries people's expectation of life was poor, and medicine was hardly holding its own against illness and disease. Even so, I would have liked living in the past, I think.'

She nodded, and sat lost in thought for a long time, her imagination fired by Clive's words. She was a romantic, as indeed were most girls, but she had always tried to separate reality and romance in her mind. Her job was such that reality stood out all the more starkly for her, and she felt that she missed a great deal of the pleasures of life because she could never quite forget that living itself was a grim affair for a great many people.

She shrugged off her thoughts and brought her mind back to the present. She looked at Clive, and studied his profile for long moments while he concentrated upon his driving. She had known him hardly more than a week now, and yet she could readily accept that he was something out of the ordinary for her. She could see it all the more clearly because of Frank Munro. Frank had come into her life in much the same way that Clive had, and yet she distrusted Frank and could not like him. Clive, on the other hand, she respected — and liked more than she cared to admit.

He was falling in love with her — that much became clear to her as she let her mind dwell on the past week. She could remember everything that had passed between them, and that day when he had first kissed her stood out in her mind like a milestone. She felt emotion stir within her at recollection of that snowy afternoon, and she reached out a gentle hand and touched his shoulder, unable to prevent herself from making contact.

Clive glanced quickly at her but he could not tell what was passing through her mind, and merely smiled as he looked ahead again.

They drove on into the country town of Inverglen, and Kay immediately saw the huge castle squatting on a massive mound overlooking the town. In her visits to her aunt and uncle, she had never come to this place, and consequently she looked around with the eyes of a stranger.

'Lunch first,' Clive said. 'The castle doesn't open until two. I'm hungry. I don't know about you, but I was so excited at the prospect of spending all day with you that I was quite unable to eat breakfast. I felt like a schoolboy about to go on some long-awaited treat.'

'Really?' She looked at him as he parked the car, and he turned to her with a sigh of relief when he'd switched off the engine.

'I ought to have made you drive,' he said. 'Then I could have sat watching you all the way. Scotland is noted for its scenery, but it has nothing to compare with you.'

Kay laughed. 'You're getting very

proficient with your compliments, Clive!'

But he was suddenly serious. 'Oh, Kay. I wish this day could go on and on without pause that we didn't have to return home tonight, to let society make its constant demands upon our time and skill.'

'That sounds bad,' she ventured. 'What's the matter, Clive? Are you letting a pretty face make you forget your duty?'

'Not at all.' He smiled as he opened the door of the car. 'I would never do that. I think it's a mistake to keep two parts of a life separate, especially in my particular vocation. I think one should complement the other.'

'If the woman is of the type to blend in,' Kay said, getting out of the car. She stood by while he locked the vehicle, and then he came to her side, taking her arm. She looked up into his face, and hardly felt the chill wind blowing against her with all the spite and malice it could muster.

'You're my type,' he said simply. 'I'd never look any farther than you, Kay.'

They walked around the shopping centre of the town, and Kay made several purchases. Clive followed her around with a good-natured smile upon his face, and it wasn't until they returned to the car that she remembered that, on their arrival, he had complained about being hungry.

'I am sorry!' she apologized. 'Why didn't you insist on going to the hotel immediately? The shopping could have waited.'

'It was too early to eat, in any case,' he retorted. 'But we shall have lunch now, before we even consider anything else. Come along.' He took her hand and led her out of the car park, and Kay was filled with pleasure at their contact.

She found that she, too, was hungry, and they both did full justice to the meal which Clive ordered. After lunch, they went for a stroll until it was time to go to the castle. Clive paid the entrance fee and they crossed the drawbridge, beneath which lay dark and placid waters. Their footsteps echoed, and the atmosphere was dank, cold and cheerless. Kay drew instinctively closer to Clive, and he tightened his grip upon her elbow as they ascended worn stone steps to enter the large keep.

The castle was in a good state of repair. There were ancient suits of armour standing in corners, and an array of old-fashioned arms fixed to the smooth stone walls. An air of timelessness seemed to pervade the many large rooms, and Kay found her imagination working overtime, prompted by the sights and smells of the building. They eventually found themselves upon the windswept battlements and there they stood, unmindful of the weather, with a commanding view of the surrounding countryside.

'This is marvellous, Clive,' Kay told him, pushing closer to him in a bid to shelter from the wind. 'No wonder you like to come here often.'

'It does something to me to walk these lonely passages and peer into the rooms,' he said softly. 'It's like looking back into the past. I do feel a morbid attraction to time gone by, and I don't know why, really. It's not that I'm dissatisfied with the present — I'm quite happy in my work — and there's you.' He smiled. 'But it's something much greater than any of this. I can't explain it, but when I go away from here I usually feel a great sense of peacefulness.'

. . . They stood together on the battlements until the cold wind got through to them. Kay looked up at the glowering sky and suppressed a shiver.

'It's getting dark even earlier this afternoon,' she commented.

'There's snow up there,' Clive said.

Even as he spoke there was a flurry of sleet, and a large flake of snow settled on Kay's nose. Clive laughed as he flicked it away, then he took her hand and hurried her to the door that led down into the interior of the castle.

'We'd better start thinking of returning to Stranduthie,' he said. 'Once it starts snowing in these parts it never knows when to stop.'

She nodded regretfully, and they left the castle. Snow was falling quite heavily by the time they drove out of town, and Clive had to switch on his lights. Kay sat silent at his side, her mind filled with strange emotions. She felt very close to him, yet she could hardly accept that he was becoming so important to her because they were still practically strangers. She had to get used to the idea of knowing him. She had always been slow to make friends because of an innate caution, but Clive was fast becoming something more than a friend, and it was so unexpected that she needed time to consider the changes taking place.

'What about next Friday?' Clive asked suddenly, and Kay jerked herself from her thoughts to smile at him.

'Are you afraid someone else will get in before you?' she countered.

'No, but I like to plan ahead. Can we make a habit of going out together on our days off?'

'I'd like that. I've really enjoyed myself today.'

Clive looked at her and smiled.

. . . When they reached Stranduthie, there was a thin covering of snow on the countryside, and the wind howled unmercifully, whirling the large flakes about with malicious fury. Kay sighed regretfully when they alighted from the car in front of the house, and Clive urged her to enter the house without waiting for him to put away the car; but she would not, and she stood by the gate while he garaged the car. When he came to her side he put his arms around her.

'Let me thank you before we go in,' she said, pushing her face into his shoulder. 'We shan't find any privacy if Frank is at home.'

'He will be, if there has been no emergency,' Clive said. 'I would take you on another drive if you want to be alone with me, but I'm afraid the weather is against us now. I'm grateful for the opportunity we were given today for getting out. It's been a very long time since I enjoyed myself even half as much.'

'Thank you for taking me,' Kay said, tilting her face towards him, and he took her into his arms and kissed her soundly, unmindful of the flurrying snow; and Kay clung to him and sighed heavily because their day together was over.

'Thank you for coming along,' he responded. 'You're such a wonderful girl, Kay. I've waited a long time to meet you.'

Clive's voice was pitched low and sounded very husky, and Kay could only half understand the vibrant emotions which passed through her. Was she falling in love with him . . . ?

They were plastered with snow when they finally entered the house. Clive chuckled as he helped her off with her coat, and Aunt Margaret appeared, because of their laughter together. The older woman stood looking at them for a moment, taking in Kay's elated mood, and she nodded knowingly as she came forward with a happy smile on her face.

'I've been thinking about you,' she said quickly. 'When it began to snow I thought of all kinds of dreadful things happening. You do hear of so many tragedies these days! But you're quite capable, Clive, I know. Nevertheless, I'm glad to see you both back home. Did you have a nice time?'

'Wonderful, Aunt!' Kay responded.

'She was a bit of a nuisance,' Clive said cheerfully. 'When we walked round the shops she was like a child, wanting everything she saw. But I soon cured her of that.'

Kay laughed, and he chuckled. Aunt Margaret nodded happily.

'It's done you both the world of good,' she declared. 'You'll feel all the better for it when you take up your duties again tomorrow. Now what about some tea? The weather has taken a turn for the worse again. Are you cold?'

'Not at all!' Kay was too exhilarated to worry about anything so trivial. 'Are you watching television? Where's Uncle Edgar?'

'We are watching television, but I'm not very interested in the programme. I'll get you some tea.'

'No, I'll do it, Aunt,' Kay said. 'You go and sit down. Would you like a cup of tea when I make one?'

'Yes, please.' Aunt Margaret nodded her understanding, and Kay smiled as the older woman turned away.

She led Clive along to the kitchen, and they closed the door after entering. Kay bade him sit down, and asked him what he wanted to eat. There was a close atmosphere of intimacy about them which came from the hours they had spent together, and Kay didn't want to lose the feeling. She could see that Clive was similarly affected, and the knowledge gave her such a sense of

well-being that she could only hope
nothing would turn up that might spoil
everything . . .

4

Kay found that her life took on a deeper meaning as the days went by and she knew that she was falling in love with Clive. She was conscious of what was happening inside her, and was surprised that it should happen so suddenly and so completely, but she welcomed the changes that were becoming apparent. She now had something to look forward to beyond duty, and her life seemed to take on a wider perspective.

Her only anxiety, at that time, was the weather. The snow which had begun falling on Friday, when Clive took her to Inverglen, continued steadily over the week-end, and by Monday morning the country roads were all but closed. When she went out to start her round, having brought her list up to date with details of new patients to visit, Kay found herself in a long line of traffic all moving in the same direction, and there was a similar line of vehicles trying to get into Stranduthie.

She sat for some time in the line, feeling exasperated as they made little progress. Her wheels spun every time she tried to creep forward with the line, and it was obvious that until a snow plough went along the roads there would be little hope of getting away from the town. At length, she turned her car out of the line, skidding badly in the process, and drove back home along streets which had been salted and were almost clear. She sighed as she left the useless car and carried her bag into the house. Her uncle appeared as she stood in the hall, and he looked surprised to see her.

'The roads are almost impassable, Uncle,' Kay said. 'How am I going to get through?'

'You'll just have to wait until the snow ploughs have been through. I have this trouble every year.' He sounded wistful for a moment. 'You'll have to start later, that's all.'

'Well, I'm not going to stand around and bite my nails in frustration,' she said.

The front door banged at that moment and she turned to see Frank Munro standing on the threshold. His face was showing anger, and Kay wondered what had happened to him, because he was supposed to be doing the rounds that day.

'Some idiot ran into me while I was waiting to get out of town,' Frank said angrily. 'The roads are like skating rinks. It seems the snow plough which is supposed to handle these local roads has broken down and won't be functioning until midday.'

'Oh, heavens! I have a confinement that won't wait,' Kay said sharply. 'I can't hang around for the road to be cleared. I'm going now.'

'But you can't, in your car,' Frank protested.

'I'm not going to use the car,' Kay said firmly. 'I'm going to use Clive's skis!' Her blue eyes shone brightly as she looked into her uncle's weathered face, and she saw a twinkle come into his eyes.

'That's certainly a bright idea,' he said, 'but you won't be able to carry your case.'

'Well, I can take my supplies out and put them in a haversack, perhaps.'

'I have a fishing haversack that would do,' Edgar said. 'I'll get it.'

He hurried away, and Kay took up her case and placed it on the hall table, opening it to check the contents.

'I think you're being foolish,' Frank said. 'Why don't you wait until the roads have been cleared?'

'Don't flap, Frank. I'll be perfectly all right,' said Kay firmly. At that moment, her uncle returned with the haversack, and she started packing her supplies into it.

'I'll get Clive's skis out for you,' Edgar said. 'This is the sort of thing I would have done when I was a young man.' He glanced at Frank. 'What are you going to do, Frank?'

'What can I do but wait for the roads to be unblocked?' Frank grinned at Kay. 'I can't ski! But if there's a sledge and a team of dogs handy, I'll have a go at using them.'

Kay smiled, and Edgar chuckled as he went to fetch the skis for Kay.

'I admire your tenacity, Kay,' Frank said. 'I think you're a wonderful girl. I'd like to get to know you better. You're not Clive's girl, are you?'

'I wouldn't know about that,' she retorted carefully. 'Clive and I are very good friends.'

'I warned you to be careful of him. He's the kind to lead you on a bit, then drop you very heavily if you show signs of getting serious.'

'I hardly know him,' Kay said slowly. 'I'm very slow to make friends.'

Frank smiled. 'Clive is a charmer. I'd hate to see a nice girl like you suffer because of him.'

'I'm sure Clive wouldn't talk about you like this.'

'Well I'm only warning you. Forget I ever spoke, if that's the way you feel about him.'

Kay finished transferring the contents of her bag to the haversack and buckled it, she slipped her head and one shoulder through the strap and let the haversack rest upon her right hip.

'I'm ready as I shall ever be,' she said thoughtfully, and glanced at her watch. 'It's time I was on the move. I ought to be in Cairnburn by now.'

Frank shook his head and shrugged, and Kay went out to the garage, where Edgar was checking over the skis.

'Are you sure you'll be able to manage?' he demanded, as she put on the skis. He handed her the alpenstocks. 'It's going to be rough out there.'

'I'll be all right. It will be just like an afternoon's pleasure.'

'I'll bring your car to you when the roads are cleared,' he promised. 'You'll go to Cairnburn first, I presume, then on to Brechnockie, won't you?'

'That's right, but you needn't bother, Uncle. I'll get along all right.'

'It won't be any bother. I've been a doctor long enough to know that a helping hand now and again can make all the difference. I'll come and fetch you in your car, if the roads are clear in time.'

'All right!' Kay smiled as she settled her haversack upon her hip. 'I'll look out for you later.'

She set off then, and felt awkward for a moment or so. Passers-by stared at her, for she was wearing her uniform, and she could imagine the thoughts passing through their minds. Soon, however, she reached the outskirts of town, and found a much longer line of traffic trying to get through on the road that led to the villages. She passed them quickly, soon finding her stride, and she saw smiles of approval on many of the faces turned towards her as she passed.

Snow began to fall again, lightly, and

Kay pushed on resolutely. She was behind schedule already, and would permit nothing to delay her further. Knowing the area intimately, she soon left the road and skimmed along quite fast across the moors. In a surprisingly short time she saw Cairnburn in the distance and put on a spurt out of sheer exuberance. She reached the village and went to the house where she had to make her first call. As she slipped off the skis at the gate, she felt a sense of achievement at having beaten the weather.

When she visited the MacBride house, where the baby was expected, she found her patient experiencing her commencing pains, and Kay was relieved when she judged that the baby would be coming along later that day.

'I'm going on to Brechnockie now, and then to Kilbernian,' she explained to Mrs. MacBride. 'After that, I shall return here. I don't think we can expect anything to start happening until early evening, Mrs. MacBride, and by that

116

time the roads should be open.'

'Shall I telephone your home if anything does start happening unexpectedly?' the woman asked.

'Please do,' Kay told her. 'I call in every so often to check, and if you leave a message I shall soon get it.'

The woman nodded, reassured, and Kay took her leave. As she skied along the village street she saw a snow plough at work, and a sigh of relief escaped her as she realized that the entire road to town would be open by noon. She went on to Brechnockie, and again took to the moors to cut out the twisting route which the road followed.

It was almost eleven when she reached Brechnockie, and although she was feeling tired from the unaccustomed exercise, she did not waste any time but made her calls. Then she telephoned home, and Aunt Margaret answered, informing her that Edgar had departed in the car and was on his way to meet her. Kay decided to wait in the village for him, and twenty minutes later he arrived.

'Hello, Kay,' he greeted, opening the boot for her to put away the skis. 'So your scheme worked well, did it?'

'Very well. My legs ache, but I made quite good time, and I shan't have to worry about the weather any more. If the roads become blocked, then I shall use the skis.'

'I'll drive you on to Kilbernian,' Edgar said with a smile. 'If you're not too long we shall be home in good time for lunch.'

They got into the car and Edgar drove carefully along the road. Kay leaned back and relaxed. Her legs were trembling now with tiredness, and she had to stifle a yawn or two as they went on.

'You're settling down very well to this work, Kay,' Edgar said suddenly. 'I've been watching you carefully for signs, and I think you're going to enjoy it here, aren't you?'

'I'm in love with the work, Uncle,' she replied.

'And in love with Clive, I shouldn't wonder,' he added.

She glanced at him quickly, caught his eye, and smiled. 'I've still got an open mind on the subject,' she said slowly. 'I have taken a great liking to Clive, that's true, but if it goes any deeper than that, I don't know yet.'

'I'm not prying. I hope something does come of your meeting with him. It would settle your aunt's mind if you fell in love with Clive — and you couldn't pick a better man.'

'What about you, Uncle?' She changed the subject adroitly. 'I think you're enjoying your rest, aren't you?'

'Yes, Kay, I am,' he said, turning to smile at her. 'More, in fact, than I thought I would. I'm already beginning to feel like a new man.'

'Well, that's good news!' As she spoke, they rounded a bend and came in sight of Kilbernian.

A few moments later, Edgar brought the car to a halt near the Post Office in the village. Kay glanced at her watch.

'I've got four calls to make here, Uncle. I won't be long.'

'I'll sit here and wait for you,' he retorted. 'Would you like me to call the house and make a check for you?'

'Yes, please! I'll come back to the car when I've done my calls and, if there are any emergencies, I'll do them afterwards.'

. . . When Kay returned to her uncle, some half-hour later, he informed her that there were no calls at home awaiting her, and she settled herself in the car and he drove her back to Cairnburn to check upon Mrs. MacBride. There were no surprises there, so they went on to town to lunch.

They went into the house, and had to relate their experiences to Aunt Margaret. Clive hadn't come in yet, but Frank Munro was waiting for lunch, and he grinned at Kay.

'I couldn't find a sledge and dog team,' he said lightly. 'I shall have to take up ski-ing. I can see that. Would

120

you care to give me a few lessons?'

'I'm afraid I don't have the time for that sort of thing,' she replied instantly, and saw him smile ruefully. 'But no doubt there are many teachers in this part of the country, and at this time of the year.'

'I can see that I've arrived here too late,' he retorted.

'For what?' she demanded.

'For getting in with you. I wish I could have met you before you met Clive.'

'What's Clive got to do with it?' she continued, determined not to give ground in any way.

'If you don't know, then it would be a complete waste of time trying to explain to you. You're a very determined woman, aren't you? The way you took to skis this morning in order to get to your patients proves that.'

'Well one should go all out for duty,' she said with a smile.

'Are you in love with Clive?' His lips twisted as he spoke.

She regarded him for a moment. Then, before she could answer, Edgar appeared in the doorway.

'Would you two like a drink before lunch?' he demanded.

'I'll have a sherry, please!' Kay said.

'Nothing for me,' Frank retorted.

'Was your car badly damaged this morning?' Edgar asked Frank.

'It will be ready for me this afternoon,' came the terse reply. 'They can't do the repairs today. They're just making it road-worthy.'

'So how did you make your calls this morning?' Kay asked him.

'I didn't. Clive did them instead.'

'That's why Clive isn't back yet,' Aunt Margaret said from the doorway. 'He telephoned a short time ago, saying that he wouldn't come in until he'd finished the house calls. But lunch is ready, and no doubt you want to get away soon afterwards, Kay. You have a Clinic this afternoon, haven't you?'

'I shall check with Mrs. MacBride

before going to the Clinic, and no doubt I'll be called away before the afternoon is over.'

They had lunch, and Kay missed Clive, although she found Frank keen to talk. She didn't have much time, but she waited as long as she dared in the hope of seeing Clive before going off about her afternoon's business. However, she had to depart in the end without seeing him.

'Aunt, tell Clive I waited as long as I could,' she said to Margaret Duncan. 'If there's a call for me from Mrs. MacBride, you'll be able to contact me at the Clinic in Cairnburn. You have the number on the pad.'

'I know the number, dear,' Aunt Margaret said. 'Off you go, and don't work too hard.'

Kay nodded and took her leave. She found there had been a little more snow during the hour or so that she had been at home, but it wasn't sufficient to prevent her using the car. She went to the Clinic and was kept very busy until almost four, when there was a telephone call for her. She expected it to be about Mrs. MacBride, and knew she was right as soon as she heard her aunt's voice. It was a message to say the woman was worried because of her pains, and Kay decided to make an immediate visit.

The roads were passable and she found little trouble in driving to Cairnburn, arriving there to find a neighbour with Mrs. MacBride. Kay examined the woman and agreed that developments were taking place. But it was still early.

'I'll go back home to pick up some equipment, and I'll be back in about an hour,' Kay promised.

'Thank you, Nurse. I'm rather nervous now.'

'There's nothing to worry about,' Kay assured her. 'I'll be back in time, don't you fear.'

Kay took with her the memory of Mrs. MacBride's smile of appreciation, and it warmed her as she set off back to town. When she reached Stranduthie it was dark, and snow was falling again. She parked the car and hurried into the house, to find Clive waiting to see her; they met in the big front sitting-room.

Clive looked tired as he got to his feet to greet her, but he smiled and took her into his arms. When he kissed her, Kay's tiredness seemed to vanish as if he had waved a magic wand over her. He looked down into her face, shaking his head slowly.

'Aunt Margaret told me all about your ski-ing episode this morning,' he said. 'I thought you were joking, that Saturday afternoon when we were out ski-ing together and I suggested that you use skis instead of the car when the weather was too bad. What was it like, anyway?'

'I was surprised I managed so well,' she told him. 'I felt tired by the time Uncle Edgar came and picked me up in the car, but it went off all right.'

'And you've got to attend Mrs. MacBride this evening, haven't you?' His tones sounded flat and unemotional, and she thought he was overtired.

'I don't mind that, although it seems to have been rather a long day already.' She sighed heavily. 'What's wrong, Clive? Have you had a hard day?'

'No harder than usual. Why do you ask?'

'You look exhausted. Do you feel unwell?'

'No.' He shook his head. 'I'm quite all right. Perhaps it is the time of year.' He smiled slowly, and she found herself thinking that he wasn't telling the truth.

'Have you had tea?' she asked. 'I've missed seeing you all day. I hung on after lunch in the hope that you would soon return.'

'I'm sorry about that, but Munro had trouble with his car and I wouldn't lend him mine. He doesn't know how to treat his own property properly, so I won't give him the chance to ruin mine. I did his calls for him.'

'I know, and expect you did too much.' Kay tried to fight down her questioning intuition, but for some unknown reason there was a nagging doubt in her mind, and the more she tried to suppress it the more insistent it became. But she didn't ask more questions of Clive because he seemed reluctant to talk about anything.

She set out after tea to the home of Mrs. MacBride with the problem of Clive and his strange behaviour still bothering her. But she soon forgot him as she concentrated on the forthcoming delivery. The baby didn't arrive until almost midnight, however, and by then Kay was too tired to let her thoughts worry her further. The drive home was tiring because there had been a fresh fall of snow, and when she finally arrived, she found the house in darkness.

Everyone had gone to bed! She smiled ruefully and left her car beside the garage, telling herself that she ought to do something about getting the vehicle under cover. Then, as she entered the house, she heard a car approaching. It turned into the alley at the side of the house where the garage was, and she hurried outside again, realizing that Clive must have been out on a call. Her car was blocking the way into the garage, and would have to be moved.

She paused at the corner of the house and saw Clive getting out of his car. There was someone with him, and Kay narrowed her eyes as she tried to pierce the gloom. Then the person with Clive turned and hurried on along the alley, making for the back road behind the house. Kay caught her breath as she watched the figure from the cover of the corner. When Clive's companion passed under a street lamp along the alley, there was sufficient light for Kay to see that the person was a woman.

Without knowing exactly why she did it, Kay turned and hurried back into the house before Clive could see her. She didn't want him to know what she had seen!

* ★ *

Kay went into the kitchen to make herself a hot drink, and her hands trembled as she set a pan of milk upon the electric stove. Shortly afterwards, she heard the front door close, and she looked out into the hall to see Clive taking off his overcoat. She sighed inaudibly as he looked at her and, in the moment before he really saw it was she, her sharp eyes noticed that his expression was harsh and set.

'Would you like some hot milk, Clive?' she asked, and it annoyed her to notice her tones wavering.

'Yes, please, if you're doing some for yourself,' he replied. 'I'll be with you in a moment.'

His voice sounded natural, and she nodded and withdrew into the kitchen again. She wondered what had arisen in her subconscious mind to make her feel so doubtful about the incident which she had witnessed. There could be a dozen reasonable explanations for the presence of a woman in Clive's car, and no doubt he would tell her about it as soon as he came to talk to her. But she could not reassure herself. She heard his footsteps outside the kitchen and, though her pulses leaped with surging excitement, she did not turn to face him as he entered the room.

'You're up late,' he remarked. 'Have you just finished?'

'I came in about ten minutes before you did,' she replied. 'I delivered Mrs. MacBride's daughter at about a quarter to midnight.' She forced a tired smile as he paused to study her weary features. 'You're out late, too,' she said.

'I had an emergency. But I was half-expecting it.' A shadow crossed his face. 'The patient died.' He sighed heavily and pulled out a chair and sat down at the table. 'It was old Mr. Hanford. I didn't give him long to live, a month ago, but he fought to the end.'

Kay could see he was upset but, for some reason, she didn't think it was because he had lost a patient. She watched his face for some moments until she had to turn quickly to the stove to rescue the milk from boiling over. She filled two beakers and turned to the table, placing one of them before him.

'Would you like something to eat?' she inquired.

'No, thank you!' His voice was still harsh. 'I'm ready for bed. I'll take this milk up with me and drink it there.' He seemed to shiver a little. 'I think I've got a cold coming,' he went on.

'Have you taken anything?' she asked.

'I'll take something when I get into bed,' he declared, getting to his feet. He looked at her for a moment, and she saw worry in his eyes. Then he moistened his lips. 'Good night, Kay. See you tomorrow. You'd better hurry up and get to bed — you're going to be awfully tired in the morning.'

'Good night, Clive.' She kept disappointment out of her tones when she realized that he was not going to kiss her. He nodded slowly, took up his beaker, and departed.

Kay took a deep breath and exhaled it slowly. She pictured again the woman she had seen hurrying along the alley, and knew it had been a young person. Clive had made no mention of her, and Kay wondered if her imagination and intuition were playing her tricks. But Clive had seemed cold and distant and, although his attitude could be accounted for, she found herself believing that there was more to it than he had said.

She sighed as she drank her milk, and then she prepared to go to bed. She fell asleep almost the instant her head touched the pillow, and the next thing she was aware of was Aunt Margaret shaking her awake.

Kay had to tell her aunt all about the MacBride case, and she sipped her tea as she recounted the incidents of the previous day. There was a flatness inside her, a sensation of dullness that didn't come just from her tiredness. She

132

thought of Clive, and knew it was not just imagination that was disturbing her — there had been some strangeness in his manner last night, and the more she thought about it the more certain she became.

'There's been a lot more snow, Kay,' Aunt Margaret said, getting up from the foot of Kay's bed to walk across the room and stare from the window. 'It looks as if you might have to use the skis again first thing.'

When Kay went down to breakfast, she found Frank Munro in the kitchen talking with Aunt Margaret, and Kay remembered Frank's words about Clive. But she didn't think there could be any truth in what the man had said — Clive was not like that. There had been a trace of envy in Frank's voice at the time, and there was every reason for Kay to doubt his words; but he looked at her keenly when she entered the kitchen and, for a moment, she fancied he knew something of what had happened last night.

But that seemed ridiculous, upon second thoughts, and she tried to force the whole upsetting situation from her mind.

'Clive said he thought he'd got a cold coming,' she said as she went to help her aunt.

'Did you see him last night?' Frank demanded. He sat opposite Kay, and his eyes were steady and intent as he regarded her.

'Yes. He came in just behind me after midnight. He attended an emergency call. Old Mr. Hanford died, I believe he said.'

'Really!' Aunt Margaret turned from the stove where she was doing toast. 'I knew the poor old man was very ill. I'm sorry to hear that!'

'Clive seemed really upset about it.' Kay was trying hard to obliterate the memory of the woman hurrying away from Clive's car. There had to be some explanation for that! The knowledge came up into the forefront of her mind and she tried to cling to it, but it proved elusive, and kept darting out of her reach despite all her efforts.

'Are you going on your skis this morning?' Frank asked her.

'I don't know. I haven't properly checked the conditions yet.'

'It's almost as bad as yesterday out there, and the weather forecast is that there's a lot more snow on the way.'

Kay nodded slowly. 'I proved to myself yesterday that I can get around on skis, so I'm not worried about the weather any more.' She suppressed a sigh as she told herself that she had acquired a far deeper worry about Clive; but she could say nothing of that. She studied Frank's face reflectively, wondering if she could ask him about Clive, and what he had meant when he talked of Clive's manner towards women, but she knew she could never broach the subject and she tried to thrust the whole idea out of her mind.

'I certainly hope you'll get through all right this morning without too much trouble,' Aunt Margaret was saying.

'I'll be able to cope,' Kay assured her, and left the kitchen.

When she left the house she found snow falling again, and she paused at the corner of the house and looked along the alley where she had seen the woman the night before. But duty was calling now and she went to her car and prepared it for travel. There was a blanket of snow upon it which had to be removed, and she took a scraper to the windows to remove the frozen condensation of the night before.

The engine started with no trouble, and she sighed with relief as she got behind the wheel and prepared herself for the day's battle against the elements. The roads in town were cleared, having been treated with salt, and as she approached the outskirts she found a line of traffic building up and knew the country roads were giving trouble. However, this time the traffic kept moving, although very slowly, and she stayed with it, keeping an eye upon her watch as she travelled farther from town.

When she reached Cairnburn she quickly made her round of the village. She found a jubilant Mrs. MacBride waiting for her and, as she bathed the baby, Kay listened to the woman's high spirited chatter, smiling to herself. This was what her job was all about! She helped people who needed her.

Kay took a deep breath and tried to throw off the yoke of foreboding that seemed to envelop her. What had made her feel like this? Her intuition had started it and, as a result, she was acting foolishly and without good reason. Yet no matter what she tried, she could not overcome her fears. She realized that she would have to broach the subject to Clive before obtaining any kind of relief — but that was something she would find very hard to do . . .

When she had finished her morning round, Kay began the drive back to Stranduthie. Snow was falling again, and she had to travel very slowly in order to see clearly. As she reached town the wind seemed to grow stronger, and the snow came storming down, cutting visibility drastically. She was thankful to get home, but even covering the short distance between the kerb and the front door, caused her to be almost completely covered in snow. She entered the hall and paused to shake the snow from her coat.

Aunt Margaret came through from the kitchen, exclaiming at the weather, and Kay heaved a long sigh of thankfulness that her country calls, barring emergencies, were over for the day.

'Has Clive come in yet?' Kay asked her aunt.

'No, he hasn't, dear,' Margaret paused for a moment, surveying her niece, then: 'Kay, would you mind if I asked you something?'

Kay's surprise showed in her voice. 'No, Aunt, of course not.'

'Well, then — how are things between you and Clive?'

138

Kay smiled ruefully. 'Why do you ask?'

'I'm worried about him,' Margaret replied simply.

'Really?' Kay's tones deepened, despite her efforts to remain unmoved. 'Why, exactly?'

'In the past two days he seems to have become moody.'

'Well, he told me last night he thinks he's got a cold coming on. Perhaps that would account for it.'

'It isn't that.'

'What reasons do you have for thinking it might be something more?'

'None at all. Intuition mostly.' Aunt Margaret shook her head slowly as she considered, and Kay smiled thinly, knowing what her own intuition had done to her peace of mind. 'Perhaps he doesn't like Frank being here in the same house with you.'

'That's ridiculous! Surely you don't believe that, Aunt?'

'Why not? Clive wasn't happy when he first learned it was Frank coming here. He said he didn't like him, that he didn't think Frank would settle into the job; and Frank had something to say about Clive, didn't he? There's some sort of a mystery in Clive's life.'

'Mystery?' Kay repeated. 'Surely not!'

'Frank talks a whole lot more to me than he does to you. It seems that Clive was thought to be the brightest student in many a long year, but something happened that put an end to his ascendancy. You couldn't say this practice was in any way progressive — so why did he come here?'

'Perhaps the scenery appealed to him!' Kay shook her head. 'There could be a hundred and one different reasons for his decision, and all of them reasonable, Aunt. I wouldn't listen too much to what Frank has to say about Clive. I get the feeling that Frank is a little bit jealous of Clive.'

'Perhaps you're right, but I can't help feeling that an atmosphere is building up here, and there's something at the bottom of it which we don't know about.'

'I can't agree with you, Aunt,' Kay said sharply. 'They seem to be getting along fairly well together to me.'

'I'm not concerned so much for their harmonious existence as for your welfare, Kay. You're the one who counts, and if it seems that you're going to be in the middle between those two, then something will have to be done about it before trouble can start.'

'Aunt, I don't understand what you're getting at. What do you mean?'

'It's simple. I think Clive fell in love with you in the week you were here before Frank arrived. Now he's afraid that Frank might get you away from him.'

'That's absurd!' Kay said sharply.

'Think about it for a moment. Clive did say that Frank was a lady-killer, as a student.' Aunt Margaret's brown eyes sparkled.

'Frank said practically the same thing about Clive!'

'Yes, he did — I remember. All the

more reason, then, to be careful how you go about things.'

'All right, Aunt dear, I'll be careful,' Kay sighed, turning towards the sitting-room. 'Now, I'm just going to sit down for a few moments before lunch. Call me if you want any help.'

'No, dear, you go and rest. Lunch won't be long.'

Kay went into the sitting-room and was about to shut the door when she heard the front door bang. She looked into the hall, and her heart skipped a beat when she saw it was Clive entering the house. His face was harshly set, and she wondered what had happened to his smile. She went forward a step so he could see her, and she was a little disappointed when his face did not alter expression at sight of her.

'Hello, Kay,' he said thinly. 'Glad to see you safely home. I had a rough morning. How did you make out?'

'Hardly any trouble,' she said lightly, going forward to help him out of his coat, and she noticed that he recoiled at her touch. Her heart sank, but she told herself that it was only her imagination. 'How is the cold?' she went on, determined not to show him that she felt something was wrong.

'It hasn't developed. Perhaps I was chilled and thoroughly tired last night.' His face hardened still more. 'Has Munro come in yet?'

'I haven't seen him. I've been in only a few minutes myself.' Kay was telling herself that he never used Frank's Christian name, and she wondered at it. 'Do you want to see him in particular?'

Her question seemed to upset Clive, and he stared at her keenly. 'No! Why should I?' he demanded.

'I thought there was a note in your voice which suggested that you did!' She smiled. 'Come in here by the fire. I was about to sit down for a few minutes before lunch. What troubles did you meet with this morning?'

'I skidded off the road twice,' he said, following her into the sitting-room. He closed the door firmly and walked across to stand before the fire.

Kay watched him, hardly recognizing him as the man of the week before. There was no warmth in his tones, and his eyes showed none of the emotion which she had become accustomed to seeing. He watched her and she met his gaze steadily.

'Do I sound bad tempered?' he asked suddenly.

'Just a bit,' she said, smiling slowly. 'Why — did you get out of bed on the wrong side this morning?'

'Not really. I never let myself become affected by small matters. I'm usually an even minded person, but today I am a bit put out, and I've got the feeling that I've been taking it out on everyone.'

'I haven't noticed any difference,' Kay lied, and saw him smile.

'You should have been a diplomat, not a nurse,' he retorted, and reached out for her suddenly, taking her by surprise. He pulled her into his arms and kissed her soundly, and Kay felt her tension flee as quickly as if it had never been.

It was all right, she told herself remotely. It had all been her imagination. He still felt very keenly about her, and what happened last night must have a simple explanation. She closed her eyes and ordered herself to forget what had happened. This was all that mattered now! While Clive could kiss her like this, then everything just had to be all right . . .

5

When Clive released her, Kay found she was almost in tears with relief, but she kept her feelings from showing in her face, and her voice was without tremor when she spoke. 'What's upset you, Clive?' she asked, knowing that she ought to show a womanly curiosity. 'It's nothing I've done, is it?'

'Of course not!' He stared into her face for a moment. 'Kay, nothing you ever did would upset me. You're the most wonderful girl in the world as far as I'm concerned. I only wish I had met you five years ago.'

'You talk as if meeting me now makes it too late!' She said the words before she realized it, and saw his features harden for a moment. Then he shook his head slowly and smiled.

'It's never too late for most things, you know,' he said seriously.

'Then you have a problem facing you?'

'It's nothing I can't handle.' His voice was low now, and he clipped his words as if he detested having to use them.

So there was something! Kay caught her breath as she thought about it, aware that he was still watching her. She forced a smile.

'Tell me if there's anything I can do to help. I'm usually pretty good at solving problems.'

'I'm sure you are,' he retorted warmly. 'But this is something I have to take care of for myself.'

At that moment, Kay heard Margaret calling from the dining-room to say that lunch was ready. She slipped her arm through Clive's and drew him towards the door. 'We'll have to go in to lunch,' she said. 'I can hear Aunt Margaret calling.'

'What are you doing this afternoon, Kay?' he asked, as he opened the door for her.

'I'm due at the Clinic. Why?'

'I thought perhaps we could spend some time together. I shall have a little time to myself directly after lunch.'

'I'm sorry, but I shall have to leave fairly soon after lunch.'

'It obviously isn't my lucky day,' Clive remarked dryly, as they entered the dining-room.

Kay laughed, but she was still uneasy. She found herself hoping that it was her imagination that had caused her worries. During the meal she studied Clive's face but, apart from a certain stiffness in his manner, he appeared no different from normal. Was she reading too much into her intuitive thoughts? She wished she could have broached the subject of the woman she had seen getting out of his car. A few words from him on the matter would probably clear the air completely, but she had that deep rooted feeling that there was more to it than there seemed to be. She held her counsel and her tongue, and could only hope that whatever it was bothering him, it would leave him in peace very soon.

Before they had finished the meal, Frank Munro entered the room. Kay watched his face as he came to the table, and she saw the strange glance that he bestowed upon Clive as he greeted them generally.

'I'd like to have a word in private with you after lunch, Munro,' Clive said sharply, in reply to Frank's greeting.

Kay saw Frank frown, but he replied pleasantly enough.

'All right, but you'll have to make it short and sweet. I shall have to dash off as soon as I've eaten'

'I can promise you it will be short, but I doubt if it will be very sweet,' Clive said. He glanced at Kay, then at Aunt Margaret, and pushed back his seat. 'Please excuse me,' he said, rising. 'I have some papers to look up before I go out this afternoon.'

Kay watched the door closing behind him, and she blinked to force away the tears that threatened to flood her eyes.

Something was seriously wrong here, and she was half afraid to try and get to the bottom of it.

'He doesn't seem to be in a very good mood,' Frank said, unabashed by the reception he had received. He grinned as he looked at Kay. 'Have you two fallen out over something, or had a lovers' tiff?'

'Certainly not!' she retorted.

'Sorry I asked.' He was mocking her, she knew, and she refused to be drawn. 'I suppose it's the weather,' he resumed. 'It is a bit depressing.'

Kay imagined that Frank was elated by Clive's attitude, and she frowned as she considered it. Was Frank deliberately inciting bad feelings? It seemed that way to her, but she could not for the life of her think why. She sighed heavily as she excused herself and left the table. She had better try to have another word with Clive before he went out. She could always talk to Frank, but she didn't think she would get the full truth from him.

Clive was not in the sitting-room when she looked in, and Kay paused in an undecided fashion in the doorway. She heard footsteps on the stairs and looked around eagerly; but it was Edgar coming down the stairs.

'Hello, Uncle,' she greeted. 'How are you feeling today?'

'Fine, Kay, just fine. What's it like outside?'

'Snowing hard, and there's a lot more to come,' she retorted. 'It's a good thing you don't have to turn out in it.'

'But you have a Clinic to attend this afternoon, haven't you?'

'Yes!' She nodded and moved to his side. 'I shan't take the car. I can always come back for it if I should need it.'

'I'm getting tired of winter now,' he said moodily, and Kay frowned as she looked into his weathered face. She saw a paleness beneath the skin, and studied his eyes in concern; but he smiled as he met her gaze. 'I'm all right, Kay. Just feeling my age, that's all.' He turned away. 'I'd better have my lunch now, or

151

I may lose the chance.'

Kay smiled and went on up the stairs to her room; she heard Clive moving around his room as she passed his door. She hesitated, and almost knocked, but thought better of it and went on. She saw it was almost time to prepare to go out, and stood by her window for some moments, just staring out at the falling snow.

The roads next day would be dreadful to drive upon, she thought remotely, as she turned away from the window to get ready — but that was tomorrow, and a lot could happen before then. She left her room, and paused at Clive's door to listen for him, but the room was silent now.

Looking into the sitting-room, she found Frank there, and he glanced up from the newspaper he was reading and grinned at her.

'After Farrell, are you?' he demanded, putting the paper aside. 'Well you're unlucky, Kay. He went out some minutes ago, and he was in a hurry, as if he were late for an appointment.'

Kay paused in the doorway and stared at him, wondering what lay behind his words, and there was a picture in her mind of the woman getting out of Clive's car. Acting upon an impulse, she went into the room and closed the door, walking across to the hearth and standing before it while she considered what to say. Frank watched her, his face showing curiosity.

'What is it you want to ask me, Kay?' he demanded.

'Ask you?' She turned to look at him.

'I know more about the situation that's developing than you do,' he retorted. 'You think you know something, but you don't, and that's worse than being certain of some of the facts, isn't it?' He chuckled, and the sound grated against Kay's nerves. 'What do you suspect, Kay? Come on, tell me!'

'Suspect?' She was aware that she kept repeating his words. 'What are you talking about, Frank?'

'You really don't know?'

'I'm certain I don't.' Kay was suddenly aware that she wanted to get away; that she didn't want to listen to this man any more. She glanced at her watch. 'It's getting late,' she said. 'I'm afraid I must go, Frank.'

'Would you like me to tell you about Clive before you go?' Frank asked abruptly, as she walked to the door.

Kay halted and faced him again, drawing a deep breath as she did so. 'Are you trying to cause trouble between Clive and myself?' she demanded sharply.

'Trouble?' He was smiling thinly, and his expression did not change. 'Now why on earth would I want to do that? I like you too much to want to do anything that might cause you pain. Why do you suspect that I'm trying to cause trouble? Is there any change in your relationship with Clive, especially since my arrival?'

'I didn't say that,' she retorted defensively.

'You don't have to say it. I can tell by your expression.'

'You're reading too much into my face,' she replied, and turned to the door.

He let her open the door before speaking again. Kay was sighing heavily as she went out, and his next words came sharply across the room, with the power of bullets.

'Clive is seeing another woman, did you know?'

She turned instantly, her face set in harsh lines, and her worst fears escaped her control and went rampaging through her mind. She shook her head in a vain attempt to stop them and almost stamped her foot.

'Why don't you stop talking nonsense and forget about your animosity for Clive?' she demanded. 'You're not a student now, Frank. You're a responsible man in a most responsible position, and what happened between you and Clive years ago has no place in this situation. Don't try to stir up old angers, no matter what they were about. We don't want anything like that here.'

Without giving him the chance to answer, she turned away and closed the door; but she was thoughtful as she went outside and started to walk to the Clinic.

When Kay reached the Clinic, however, she found relief in following the routine. With mothers and babies to handle, she felt her thoughts receding, and for a time she was thoroughly happy with what she was doing.

Then Nurse Harmon walked in, and the other staff crowded around the retired nurse and questioned her unmercifully. Eventually Nurse Harmon came to Kay, and they chatted for ten minutes.

'How are you enjoying your retirement?' Kay asked her.

'I'm beginning to miss the routine already, I can tell you. If I don't go out from the house, then I never see a soul all day long. You know, I would dearly love to come on your rounds with you one day, Kay.'

'I'd love to take you along, but the

weather isn't suitable at the moment.'

'I heard that you did part of your round on skis,' Nurse Harmon said with a smile. 'I like that kind of determination. It's the sort of thing I would have done.'

They talked about the patients, and Nurse Harmon asked after a great many of them. Kay could see that the old lady was enjoying herself and re-living some of her past life in her questions. Some of the mothers coming in with their babies exclaimed at seeing her, and crowded around her. Kay watched with a smile on her face, and wondered if she, too, would receive such a warm welcome after her duty was done. She began to feel wistful, and tried to shake it off, but the more she fought against it the less chance she had of beating it.

When the Clinic was finished, she telephoned her aunt and found there had been no calls for her. Telling her aunt that she was on her way home, she departed from the Clinic and began the long walk.

She wanted to try and think out the situation that seemed to be developing round her. Broadly, there was a great turmoil, but when she tried to dissect the situation there was nothing she could really put a finger on. The only disquieting fact was the incident of the woman getting out of Clive's car that night. But thinking about that did not help, although she could not discover anything directly responsible for her feelings. Her intuition had plumped for suspicions, and there had to be a reason for that.

She began to realize that jealousy was her trouble, and the knowledge hurt her as it became slowly apparent. But where there was jealously, surely there was love!

The snow seemed to come down even more heavily, and there were several inches underfoot already. Kay dared not think about the next day, when she would have to go out around the villages. She had difficulty in keeping her feet now, and the traffic was travelling very slowly on the salted roads, where snow was accumulating, despite the salt.

Then she spotted Clive's car, and she paused on a corner as it went by, her heart in her mouth, one hand half lifted to wave to him. But he didn't see her, such was his concentration upon the bad road conditions, and Kay sighed heavily. Then she saw a figure in the front passenger seat of the car as it disappeared amidst the whirling snow. Her heart seemed to freeze, and she peered intently as she tried to identify the figure. It was a woman, she saw in that split second — but that was all she could see before the car disappeared into the murk.

Kay stood motionless, oblivious of the falling snow, and she seemed as cold inside as she was out. Ice seemed to gather around her heart and she took a deep breath that filled her lungs with a deadly chill.

That woman in the car with Clive was the one who had been with him that night. She was positive! Now what could she think? The first time it might have been a woman to whom he had given a lift, perhaps someone who had visited the patient he had seen. But this second time seemed to suggest something else and Kay hardly dared let her mind dwell on it, as she stood lost in her shock and her fear.

Is wasn't until someone loomed up out of the snow and almost bumped into her that she continued her way home, but her thoughts were far from herself, and she stumbled and slithered along the ghostly pavements as if her wits had left her. Now there seemed to be some truth in the insinuations that Frank Munro had made, and Kay was desperately afraid to face up to them.

★ ★ ★

When Kay arrived home she looked for Clive's car in the garage, and was half relieved to find that it wasn't there. She was afraid to face him, in case he had something unpleasant to tell her. She stood on the corner near the house for some moments, reluctant to enter because she knew her attitude and trembling manner might betray her to Aunt Margaret's keen eyes.

She entered the house silently, hoping to divest herself of her coat and sneak up to her room without being seen, but the strong wind caught the door before she could close it gently and slammed it with such a crash that the sitting-room door shook noisily. Before she could get out of her coat, Aunt Margaret appeared from the sitting-room, and Kay made a great effort to clear her face of expression and put on a smile as she faced her aunt.

'Kay, you look like a snowman!' Aunt Margaret declared. 'I'm glad you're home. The weather is worse now than it has been all day. How have you been getting on?'

'Not too badly.' Kay forced some life into her tones. She gave an account of her afternoon while she removed her outer clothes and shook some of the snow off her coat at the door. But she kept her eyes from her aunt's face, and was glad that the cold weather had put colour into her cheeks.

'Come into the sitting-room and get warm by the fire,' Aunt Margaret said fussily.

'I feel as warm as toast,' Kay protested. 'Has Clive been home this afternoon?'

'No. He telephoned about an hour ago to say that he would go straight to the surgery without coming in for tea. He had an extra call to make.'

'Then he won't be home until seven at the earliest, will he?' Kay glanced at her watch.

'No, he won't, which is rather a pity, really.'

'Why do you say that?'

'It's just that I have two tickets for the theatre which I won't be using, and

162

I thought you and Clive might like to go. But it looks as if Clive is going to be too busy for the theatre.'

Kay recalled the brief glimpse which she'd had of Clive as he'd driven by, and she saw again the indistinct shape of the woman passenger at his side.

'He had a cold coming on last night, and I don't think he would like the theatre, anyway, to judge by the mood he seems to be in,' Kay said slowly. 'Shall we go, Aunt? I know you like the theatre, and Uncle Edgar won't want to turn out.'

'That weather out there is more than I would care to challenge tonight, Kay,' Aunt Margaret said quickly. 'But you can go if you like.'

'I might do that.' Kay nodded slowly. She felt that she had been too closely bound to duty. There was a sense of frustration in her that afforded her no peace of mind, and she had the feeling that she must do something to break the monotony.

'I wish you would. I think you're

working far too hard, you know, Kay. You're not used to this sort of life. I know your work in the hospital was very demanding, but this sort of thing is entirely different, and you've not given yourself a chance to really settle in yet.'

'I'm as settled as I shall ever be,' Kay said with a thin smile. They entered the room and she saw Edgar seated in one of the big easy chairs. He got up when he saw her, and pulled a chair forward to the fire. 'Please don't disturb yourself for me, Uncle,' she said quickly.

'You need someone to fetch and carry for you after being out in that weather all day,' he retorted. 'Come and sit down, my dear. I feel like an old fraud when I look at you and think of your day's activities while I've either been lying in bed or roasting slowly before the fire.'

'You've done more than your share of answering calls, Uncle,' Kay said, dropping thankfully into her seat and leaning forward to spread her hands to the blazing fire. Before she had been there a minute, however, there was the sound of the front door slamming, and she knew that Frank Munro had come home. He was the last person she wanted to see and she immediately got up again, saying: 'I think I'll go up to my room for a short while.'

Aunt Margaret looked at her in concern. 'What's the matter, Kay? Are you feeling unwell?'

'No. I'm perfectly all right, Aunt. But it has been a long day.'

'Then why don't you go to the theatre tonight. You're not likely to have an emergency call, are you?'

'No. There are no confinements on schedule this week.' Kay felt attracted by the idea of going to the theatre. 'Perhaps I will use one of those tickets you have, Aunt.'

'That's better! Then if Clive comes home early enough and learns that you're at the theatre he'll probably come and join you.'

Kay didn't think that was likely, although she said nothing, and they went out into the hall where Frank was taking off his coat.

'Tea ready?' he demanded.

'In a few minutes,' Aunt Margaret told him. 'What sort of an afternoon have you had, Frank?'

Kay left them talking and hurried up the stairs to her room. She had decided to go to the theatre, and she began to change, wanting to get out of her uniform as quickly as possible. A strange mood seemed to settle upon her, and she realized that it stemmed from uncertainty. She didn't know what was going on in Clive's life, and she dared not take steps to find out.

When Aunt Margaret called her to tea, Kay almost refused, not wanting to join them at the table; but then she saw how rude it would look. When she went down, she found Frank already at the table. He got to his feet at her entrance, his eyes watching her closely.

'Not running a temperature, are you?' Frank demanded as she joined them at the table.

Edgar studied her with intent gaze. 'I think you're doing too much, Kay,' he said at length.

'Nonsense,' she retorted, forcing a smile. 'The fact that I feel like going out after tea should set your minds at rest about my day's work. If I were doing too much work, I certainly wouldn't feel like going out.'

'Where are you going?' Frank asked quickly.

'To the theatre!' Kay said it in a tone which she hoped would discourage him from asking further questions, and she was relieved when he went on with his tea.

'Why don't you go with her, Margaret?' Edgar demanded as they resumed their meal.

'I don't really feel like turning out in this weather,' Aunt Margaret replied.

'Is there a spare ticket then?' Frank's eyes glistened as he looked around the table.'

'There is,' Aunt Margaret said instantly, without glancing at Kay. 'It's a pity that it's got to be wasted.'

'Isn't Clive taking you then?' Frank's eyes held Kay's glance against her will. She shook her head, unable to find her voice. 'Well, I'm available,' he went on quickly. 'Don't let's waste the ticket — I feel as if I could do with a night out.'

All eyes were upon Kay, she realized, and she took a deep breath as she tried to find the words to refuse. She saw Frank watching her with an amused gleam in his eyes, and when she thought of Clive her mind seemed to die. He was seeing a woman and keeping it a secret! So why shouldn't she go to the theatre with Frank?

'All right,' she said. 'It would be a pity to waste the other ticket.'

By the time they were ready to leave she felt less like going out than she had done previously, but she could see that Frank was greatly excited about the evening and she hadn't the heart to call it off. They went in his car, although the roads were bad.

Kay began by feeling rather awkward

in Frank's company, but he was cheerful and talkative and, by the time they reached the theatre, she was feeling more at ease.

'Shall we have a drink before going in to our seats?' Frank asked, as they entered the theatre.

'I don't think so,' Kay replied in level tones.

'Come on,' he said quickly, grinning at her. 'You don't have to be uppity just because I'm offering to buy you a drink. I'm only trying to be friendly.'

'Am I being unfriendly towards you?' she demanded in turn.

'You're not unfriendly, but you're not friendly, either. You're rather cold towards me, Kay, and I can't help wondering why.'

'It must be your imagination because I can't find any unfriendliness inside me at this moment,' she said.

'It's not imagination. I suspect that it's because you're in love with Clive, and I have said some rather disparaging things about him from time to time.'

'Why?' she demanded instantly. 'What is there about Clive that you don't like?'

'Who says I don't like him?' he countered.

'You don't have to say it. It's there like a big sign hanging round your neck.'

'I'm sorry if that's the way it seems! I don't intend to show it, and I do have my reasons for not liking him. Apart from that, I was always a little bit envious of him. I came up the hard way and qualified despite all the drawbacks, but Clive Farrell had it easy, with everything going for him. It's only natural to be envious of a man like that. On top of it all, he took the girl I loved away from me.'

Kay suppressed a gasp, and looked into his eyes to see if he were joking. His eyes were narrowed, as if he were re-living that past disillusionment, and his face showed sadness.

'Let's go and have that drink,' he said rather harshly, and Kay did not object when he took her arm and led her into the bar.

Frank said no more about Clive then, and seemed rather morose during the rest of the evening. Kay found she could raise little enthusiasm for the play they watched, and afterwards found it difficult to remember what it had all been about. They went home in silence, and even the falling snow failed to evoke any comment from either of them.

When they reached the house, Kay waited for Frank to put away his car; then he came back to her where she stood sheltering from the driving snow by the corner of the house. He took her arm and walked her to the front door and, as they went inside, Kay said:

'Thanks for your company, Frank.'

He looked at her ferociously. 'You were wishing all evening that it was Clive instead of me,' he said sharply. 'I didn't enjoy myself at all. I don't suppose you did.'

'Well, don't be so upset about it. You

were insistent upon going with me. You must have seen that I didn't want you to.' Kay could begin to feel her control slipping, and she turned away and went up the stairs to her room, where, a few moments later, Aunt Margaret found her.

'Did you have a nice time, dear?' she asked.

'Not very,' Kay replied, shaking her head and smiling ruefully. 'I thought it would be a mistake to go with Frank. In future, I shall be ruled by my own judgement.'

'You would have been happier if Clive could have taken you, no doubt.'

'That's right. Has he been home this evening, by the way?'

'I haven't seen him. He telephoned to find out if there were any calls for him, and I had one emergency for him. I haven't heard from him since, and there have been no more calls.'

'I see.' Kay pictured Clive's face, and wondered again what could have happened to change their personal situation so quickly. That mystery woman riding around in Clive's car seemed to be the key to everything, and Kay wished she could find out, without asking Clive himself, just who she was. 'I'm going to bed now, Aunt,' she said slowly. 'I'm thoroughly tired out tonight.'

'It must be the weather,' Margaret said, smiling ruefully. 'Frank's already gone to bed, too, and, to judge by the way he slammed his door, he's in some kind of mood. You really dislike him, don't you, dear?'

'I suppose I do, Aunt,' said Kay simply. 'He's done nothing but be unkind about Clive since he's been here.'

'All's fair in love and war!' the older woman quoted.

'You're not going to tell me that Frank might be interested in me!' Kay stared at her aunt with disapproval on her face.

'There's more in this business than meets the eye,' Margaret said sharply.

'I'd give a lot to know what went wrong between Frank and Clive when they were younger.'

'I could tell you,' Kay said, but she shook her head. 'I don't want to discuss it, Aunt. Let sleeping dogs lie! That's the best thing to do, in this case. Perhaps they'll get over it.'

'I can't help thinking that, whatever happens, you'll come off worse than either of them,' Aunt Margaret said. 'I'll leave you now, dear. Good night. See you in the morning. By the look of the night, I'd say you'll have to use the skis tomorrow.'

'I'm looking forward to it,' Kay said.

Aunt Margaret departed and Kay sighed heavily. She undressed and prepared for bed mechanically, then, switching off the light, she got into bed and closed her eyes resolutely. Despite the turmoil in her mind, however, she fell asleep almost immediately, to awaken the following morning with a slight headache and a sense of extreme frustration.

She discovered her bad feelings when she went along to the bathroom and found the door locked against her. Frank was inside, singing, and she frowned as she recalled his bad mood of the evening before. Her own impatience flared and it was all she could do to prevent herself hammering on the door, but she turned away instead and, as she reached the door of her room, Clive's door opened, and he appeared.

'Good morning!' Kay was surprised that her tones sounded so normal, and she spoke lightly, despite her feelings.

'Hello, Kay!' He spoke heavily, and paused to look at her keenly. She studied his face and thought he looked ill.

'Are you all right, Clive?' She went closer to him, peering into his face, and he smiled slowly.

'Yes, I feel fine,' he replied. 'Why do you ask? Do I look ill?'

'You look fairly well, but there's a shadow in your eyes that wasn't there a few days ago,' she said fearlessly. 'You're overworking, or worrying badly about something.'

'A doctor always has something to worry about,' he retorted, smiling.

'Well, I don't like the look of you,' she said.

'I thought you did!' He stared at her for a moment, his smile falling away, and he seemed to tense.

'I didn't mean it like that, silly!' She smiled, despite the gravity of her thoughts, and felt the sudden desire to tell him of her fears. But then he spoke, and the opportunity fled with the change of subject.

'I understand that you went to the theatre last night with Munro.'

'That's right, and I didn't enjoy it a bit. I wish you had taken me.' She looked into his face, trying to will him to revert to his former cheery self, but he didn't seem to get the message, and she sensed that he was becoming even more remote as he watched her.

'I didn't have the time yesterday,' he

176

said. 'I was busy all day.'

'I guessed as much.' The opening was there again, Kay sensed, but she could not find the courage to broach the subject of that woman. He might tell her things that she had no wish to know. While she held hopes that nothing had changed between them, then there was a chance that everything would work out but, if she forced the issue and he turned away from her, she would never be able to face the bleak knowledge that they were through almost before they had begun.

'What are you thinking about?' he demanded.

'About my day's rounds.' Kay smiled, as she turned to the window on the landing and pulled aside the curtain to discover that almost a foot of snow had fallen during the night. 'It looks like ski-ing weather again.'

He came to stand at her shoulder, and she glanced up at him as he peered through the window. She caught the tang of his after-shave lotion, and her throat constricted. Had another woman been in his arms last night? The thought sent a pang through her which twisted her heart, and she cringed inwardly at the pain.

He looked down at her after inspecting the scenery outside. They were standing very close, and she heard him catch his breath. She resisted the impulse to throw herself into his arms, but she did reach out and place a hand against his shoulder.

'Be very careful today, Kay,' he said huskily. 'Conditions out there will be chaotic.'

'I'll be all right. You'll take care, won't you?'

'It doesn't matter about me!' There was a grim note in his tones which did not escape her, and she frowned as she moistened her lips.

'Don't be silly,' she said sharply. 'It matters a great deal to me.'

'Really?' He smiled slowly. 'I thought perhaps you were becoming interested in Munro.'

'You know that's not true. I've never lightly become interested in any man; under no circumstances did I wear my heart on my sleeve. When I came here and met you, something seemed to happen to me inside.' She fell silent and bit her lip. 'But it doesn't seem to be working out as we expected, does it?' she added.

He shook his head and his face was harsh with lines of worry.

'I just don't know what to think,' he said, shaking his head. He glanced at his watch. 'Look, I have to go out now. I can't delay any longer, Kay, but I have the feeling that I'm not being fair to you. Let's have a chat later, when I can find the time. I'll try and clear the air. I can tell by your manner that you've noticed a change in me over the past two days.'

'I have.' She nodded hesitantly, half afraid of what she might learn. 'But if it's none of my business, then you don't have to tell me about it.'

'I want it to be your business,' he said

fiercely. 'I wanted that right from the start.' He sighed again and lifted a hand, to place it heavily upon her shoulder. 'I'll try and see you later on,' he promised. 'I must have time to think. Don't go out with Munro this evening, will you?' There was something of a plea in his tones.

'I shall never go out with him again,' Kay retorted, and she shook her head as Clive nodded and turned away.

He hurried down the stairs and she went slowly into her room, alternating between hope and fear. She had the feeling that these next few days might have the power to change her life . . .

6

Kay set out on her skis, without bothering to go out and check the weather more closely; she found conditions very bad, and it was obvious that she wouldn't have got very far in the car. She skied quickly towards Cairnburn, but her thoughts were hardly upon her duty or her destination — she was trying to think round the situation as she saw it. However, no matter what she decided lay at the root of Clive's troubles, she could not account for the woman she had seen riding in Clive's car. How could one explain such an incident?

Coming out of her reverie, Kay looked around in some surprise to find that she had almost reached the village of Cairnburn. Snow was beginning to fall again, though lightly, and the wind was keen. She felt an impatience to get finished stealing through her, and resisted the impulse to put every effort into her ski-ing. She had a long way to go before the round would be over, and she had to take precautions against over-extending herself. It wouldn't help anyone if she became exhausted before the day was over and her duty was done.

Cairnburn was reached and she went along to Mrs. MacBride's home to bath the baby. She felt her usual cheerful self while she was working, and she found that she was unconsciously trying to lengthen her visits as she made her round. But time was her enemy, particularly when she didn't have her car, and she finished her calls in the village and prepared to go on to the next.

By the time she reached Brechnockie she was tired, and she half wished she had made some arrangement with Edgar to come and pick her up with the car, as he had done on the other occasion. However, where the snow plough had cleared the thicker snow away there was a thin film of hard-packed snow that was slippery, and she found it much easier to ski.

When she came out of a patient's house in the village she saw Frank Munro's car outside; he seemed to be waiting for her, evidently having seen her skis propped up by the gate. She could see that he was watching her, and he grinned as he alighted from the vehicle.

'How are you making out?' he demanded.

'Not too badly. I've been through Cairnburn and I've just finished here. I'm on my way to Kilbernian now. When I get through there, I shall be finished with calls for the day.'

'Lucky you. But jump in and I'll drive you to Kilbernian. I'm on my way there now. If you're not too long in the village I'll wait for you and drive you back to town. That will save you a lot of exercise.'

'Thanks. I'm beginning to feel the

pace,' she confessed.

During the drive to Kilbernian, Kay relaxed a little. Her legs were aching and she felt tired, but she was pleased with herself for making the effort to get through, despite the weather. She found herself staring at Frank, watching him as he concentrated on trying to control the car. He must have sensed that she was staring at him for he suddenly glanced at her and surprised her.

'What's the trouble?' he demanded. 'You're looking at me as if you've never seen anything so horrible before in your life.'

'Sorry. I was thinking, and didn't realize that I was staring at you.'

'You don't like me, do you?'

'I have no reason to dislike you, have I? Why should I not like you? You came here to relieve my uncle. You're almost a stranger to me, and you've certainly done nothing to make me dislike you.'

'But I have the feeling that you almost hate me.' He smiled as he glanced at her again. 'It's because of

184

Clive, isn't it? I said some nasty things about him and, if you're in love with him, then I suppose it's only natural you would resent anything I said to his detriment. I must admit that I have been trying to put you against him, and only because he took my girl away from me.'

'That's a strange statement to make,' Kay said. 'How can a man take a girl away from another man? Surely the girl herself chooses which man she wants?'

'I suppose so. But it wasn't for Clive himself that she went to him. It was because his prospects were so very much better than mine. He was a boy wonder — nothing short of brilliant — but it didn't work out as expected and now he's on the same level as me.' Frank shook his head slowly.

'You told me that Clive was always chasing after girls,' Kay said quietly. 'Was that true?'

'No!' Frank smiled thinly as he shook his head. 'That was a part of my attempt to drive a wedge between you.

That girl he took from me — ' he broke off and smiled thinly — 'sorry, I mean the girl who preferred him to me was about the only one he had time for when he was a student.'

'What happened to her, then?' Kay was thinking of the woman she had seen in Clive's car the day before.

'I couldn't say! This was quite some time ago. I did hear that they were to be married, but it's obvious that the wedding did not take place.'

'I saw a woman in his car yesterday!' The words came out before Kay could stop them.

'A woman!' He spoke sharply, and Kay, looking ahead, saw the houses of Kilbernian just visible. 'When was this? What did she look like?'

'I couldn't tell you what she looked like, but I was walking home from the Clinic yesterday afternoon when they passed me in his car.' Kay felt a tremor pass through her as she spoke. She didn't know how much Frank knew about Clive's business, but she found herself hoping that a miracle would occur and that he would be able to tell her that it was nothing at all to worry about. While she waited for him to comment she watched his face, and saw calculation in his expression. To her surprise, he changed the subject.

'You'd better hurry if you want a lift back to Stranduthie,' he said, drawing in to the kerb.

'Have you many calls to make?' Her mind returned to earth and she considered her duty.

'Three, but I'll wait for you, if you're not too long.'

'Thank you. I have several calls to make, but I won't keep you waiting, Frank.'

He nodded and alighted, taking with him his black medical bag, and Kay consulted her notebook before planning her route through the village.

She had a lot to think about while she did her duty, and she felt a pang of nervousness strike through her when she thought ahead to the evening. Clive had said he would talk to her, and from the way he spoke she had gathered that he meant to try and explain his attitude of the past few days. That meant he would almost certainly talk about the woman who had been in his car, and Kay felt afraid as she imagined that he was going to tell her it was all off between them. That was the worst possible thing that could happen, she thought, and tried to strengthen herself to take the blow which she was certain had to come . . .

Frank was waiting for her in the car when Kay returned to the vehicle, and she thankfully slid into the front passenger seat. He fixed her with a stare and raised an eyebrow.

'All done now?' he demanded.

'Yes, thank you! It was good of you to wait for me.'

'I haven't been waiting long. I couldn't go off knowing you would have to ski all the way back to town.'

He started the car and drove on, and Kay settled in her seat with a sigh of relief. They were silent until they reached town, and when they stopped at the house Kay glanced at her watch. They had made fairly good time, but were later than usual for lunch and, when she looked for Clive's car and failed to see it, she didn't know whether to be pleased or not. She was surprisingly nervous about meeting him for fear of what he might have to tell her.

Kay ate lunch with Frank, hoping that he might start talking again, but he said nothing during the meal, and they adjourned to the sitting-room where she picked up a magazine to read. She had barely settled herself by the fire when the door opened and Edgar came in. He greeted them both cheerfully, and Kay lowered her magazine and studied him.

'How are you today, Uncle?' she demanded.

'I'm feeling fine. The rest is doing me good. What kind of a day have you had?'

Kay told him, then her eyes went to Frank, who had muttered a greeting when Edgar entered the room and then returned to his newspaper. But she could see that he was not reading — he was watching them, his eyes narrowed, his manner intent. When silence fell, Frank moved uneasily in his seat then cleared his throat.

'Doctor,' he said rather sharply, and Edgar turned to him. 'I have to tell you that I cannot stay on here as your locum.'

Kay frowned at the words. Frank's face was set, his lips rather thin.

'What's the trouble?' Edgar asked, sitting down on a high-backed chair near Kay. 'Is there a problem?'

'It's something that's come up in the past few days, and it's personal. Would there be a possibility of your getting someone else in?'

'Of course. When do you want to leave?'

'As soon as possible. It's imperative!'

'I could always go back to work

190

myself,' Edgar said musingly. 'Would you stay until the end of the week?'

'Of course. That's the least I can do.'

'Very well! I'll set the wheels in motion immediately to find a replacement. I'm sorry about this; you were settling in quite well.'

'I know, but circumstances are against me. I must leave as soon as possible.'

'I'll make a few telephone calls immediately,' Edgar said, getting to his feet. He glanced at Kay as he went to the door, and she shrugged slightly to indicate that she had no idea what had brought this about.

When Edgar had departed, she looked at Frank again, and saw an expression of defiance upon his face. 'May I inquire as to the reason for this?' she demanded.

'I said it was personal.'

'I know you did, but I can't help feeling that it has something to do with me. Clive was looking for you a couple of days ago with a very severe expression on his face. Did he ever catch up with you for a chat?'

'It was hardly a chat!' Frank smiled thinly. 'But you're quite mistaken — it had nothing whatever to do with you.' He smiled again. 'It had nothing to do with me, either, as a matter of fact, although he wouldn't believe it.'

Kay shook her head, unable to make anything of his words. 'Is there anything I can do to help you?' she asked finally, and Frank looked up at her in some surprise.

'What could you possibly do to help me?' he demanded.

'I don't know. That's why I'm asking. I don't know what the trouble is, do I?'

He put aside the newspaper and got to his feet.

'I hardly know what it is all about myself,' he said roughly, and left the room.

Kay sat staring into the fire, feeling drowsy now, but her mind still harped on this new development. Nothing was simple, she told herself, leaning back in the seat and settling herself more comfortably. She closed her eyes and began to drift into slumber, feeling very tired, and she knew no more until Aunt Margaret came into the room rather noisily, unaware that Kay was asleep. Kay started up at the noise and gazed instantly at her watch, but was unable to see the time for a moment.

'I'm sorry, dear. I didn't know you were asleep,' Aunt Margaret said.

'I'd better get ready to go along to the Clinic,' Kay said, getting unsteadily to her feet. 'It's a good thing you came in when you did.'

'Clive just telephoned. He said it's too late for him to come in to lunch, so he's eating out. But what about Frank? Do you know what the trouble is with him?'

'I have no idea!' Kay shook her head. 'He as good as told me to mind my own business when I asked him.'

'He was settling in so well, too! I'd give a lot to know what upset him.'

Kay thought she could guess, but she

said nothing. She started to the door, wanting to freshen herself before going to the Clinic, but she paused and looked into her aunt's concerned face.

'Uncle Edgar isn't going back into the practice, is he?' she demanded.

'He'll have to, if Frank decides to leave at the week-end and there's no one to replace him!'

'I think it might help if I spoke with Clive,' Kay said slowly. 'Have you any idea which restaurant or hotel he might choose for his lunch?'

'Probably the Two Bears Hotel. He's been there before.'

'Then I'll look in on him now, and try and have a chat with him. I can't help feeling that all this has something to do with me.'

'With you?' Aunt Margaret raised her eyebrows. 'What on earth do you mean?'

'I don't know, and I wish I did! But my intuition rarely plays me false. I'll find Clive and talk frankly to him. If I can get to the bottom of it, we may be able to prevent Frank leaving, and then Uncle Edgar will be all right.'

'Don't go and ruin any chances you might have for future happiness, whatever you do, Kay,' Aunt Margaret implored.

'Uncle Edgar's life is more important than my future happiness,' Kay retorted firmly, and she meant it . . .

When Kay saw Clive's car outside the Two Bears Hotel, she felt a moment of panic, for she knew that she could not put off facing him with the problems which were daily growing larger. She went into the hotel and stood in the doorway of the dining-room, looking across the closely set tables until she spotted Clive in a corner, and her heart began to pound furiously when she saw that he was not alone. There was a woman with him!

Kay fell back a step, to remain unobserved. She stared at the woman, who was about her own age, and told herself this was the person who had been in Clive's company on the two occasions Kay had seen him with a woman. But who was she? Kay took a deep breath as she fought to control herself, but she knew she could not face Clive under these circumstances, no matter how urgent it seemed to be. She would have to wait for the evening.

There was a great confusion inside her as she went on to the Clinic but, once there, she found relief in her work. Nevertheless the afternoon was the worst she had ever experienced. Time seemed to drag and she could not concentrate properly upon what she was doing. Now she was not concerned so much for herself, however, as for Uncle Edgar. If he resumed work the effort would probably kill him, and Kay knew that, whatever the cost to herself, she must do all she could to prevent that eventuality.

When it was time for her to go home, she found a great reluctance to do so. She was not a moral coward, but what she had to do might spoil her chances for future happiness, as

Aunt Margaret had so rightly pointed out. Yet her happiness, weighed against Uncle Edgar's life, did not seem so important, and she went home, although her steps lagged and she felt less and less like meeting Clive the nearer she got.

'I'm so glad you're home, Kay,' Aunt Margaret said worriedly, as Kay came through the front door. 'Edgar has had to take the surgery this evening.'

'Why? What's happened?' Kay went to her aunt's side and placed a hand upon her shoulder.

'Frank has gone! He packed his bags this afternoon and went off just like that.'

'Oh, heavens!' Kay was shocked. 'Does Clive know about this?'

'Yes. He telephoned not long after you had left for the Clinic, and I told him that Frank was thinking about leaving. That was before Frank decided to go immediately. Clive said he'd do the rest of the house calls and, by the time he came in to collect the list,

Frank had packed and gone.'

'Is Uncle Edgar upset?' Kay demanded.

'He isn't very pleased!'

'Did he have any luck this afternoon in finding someone to take Frank's place?'

'No! He rang a number of places, but couldn't get satisfaction. I'm afraid he'll forget all about his good intentions to rest now and start working as hard as he ever did.'

'Well, I have no idea what happened to make Frank run out like that, but I'll get to the bottom of it when I talk to Clive. I shan't take less than a full explanation from him, no matter how it affects me.' Kay spoke firmly. 'Uncle Edgar's health is more important than anything.'

'Come and have tea, although I don't suppose you feel very much like it.'

'I'd better have something,' Kay said. 'I'm half expecting to be called out to a confinement some time tonight — Mrs. Cummins in Kilbernian.'

Aunt Margaret sighed. 'My poor dear! You do have to work hard, don't you? Come on, we'll have tea in the kitchen.'

Half an hour later, when she had finished her tea, Kay went to the sitting-room and sat there, waiting for Clive's return. She hadn't been there long when the telephone rang, and she hurried in answer, thinking it might be Clive ringing to say that he wouldn't be home yet.

'Nurse Whittaker?' a man's voice demanded. 'This is Mr. Cummins, of Kilbernian. You're expecting a call about my wife, aren't you?'

'Yes, Mr. Cummins. What's happening?' Kay suppressed a sigh.

'She's had three pains now, at half-hourly intervals, Nurse, and she thinks it's time you knew about them.'

'Very well, Mr. Cummins. I'll be out to see her within the hour,' Kay told him, and replaced the receiver.

The front door opened at that moment and Kay turned swiftly, her breath catching in her throat — but it was Edgar coming in, and he slammed the door wearily and paused to take off his coat. He swayed as he removed his outer garments, and Kay went to his side, taking the coat from him.

'Are you all right, Uncle?' she demanded.

'Surely,' he replied, although he was breathless and breathing heavily. 'I'm a little bit shaken because a car skidded in front of me in the High Street, and I only just managed to avoid running into him. He finished up in a shop window, and I had to give him first-aid for facial cuts. It isn't fit for anyone to be out on a night like this.'

Kay nodded understandingly as she helped her uncle into the sitting-room and then poured him a strong brandy. She would have preferred not to go out herself that evening, but she had no option, unfortunately.

She put on her coat in the hall, checked the contents of her bag, then went in search of her aunt. She would dearly have loved to discuss the situation with Clive, but that would have to wait. She found Margaret in the kitchen.

'I'm off now, Aunt,' she said. 'How is Uncle?'

'He'll be all right if he rests. But he won't be if he can't stay away from the practice.'

'Tell Clive where I've gone when he gets in, will you?' Kay hesitated over his name, and she felt confused as she turned away. 'I don't know when I shall get back, but don't worry about me — I shall be all right.'

'Have you got everything you need?' Aunt Margaret asked, following her to the door.

'Yes. I've checked everything. Good-bye until later.' Kay opened the door and departed without looking back, and her aunt closed the door behind her.

The night was very cold, and there was a light smattering of snow everywhere. Kay started the car easily enough, and she shivered, despite her heavy coat, as she drove through the town to take the road that led to Kilbernian. Presently, however, the car heater began to take effect and she shrugged her shoulders as warmer air began to circulate. The roads were still very treacherous — in some places covered with a thin film of ice — but the snow ploughs had done their work well and Kay managed to reach Kilbernian in under the hour, despite one or two bad skids on the way.

She sat for a few moments in the car, outside the Cummins's house, trying to relax after the strain of the long and exhausting drive; then she lifted her bag from the back of the car and climbed out. Jock Cummins opened the front door in answer to her knock.

'Thank goodness you're here, Nurse,' he said with relief. 'We were beginning to think you wouldn't make it!'

'There were times when I thought I wouldn't, too,' said Kay, with a laugh. 'Now, would you take me up to your wife, please, Mr. Cummins.'

When she had checked her patient, Kay found that the baby was likely to be born within the next few hours, so, to help Mrs. Cummins relax, she sat with her and her husband, telling them of some of the incidents on her drive to them, while they drank a cup of tea.

'This is a dreadful job for you, Nurse,' Jock Cummins said, shaking his head. 'It isn't fit out there tonight for a dog.'

'Well, it's my job, and I have to do it,' Kay retorted. She smiled as she got to her feet. 'I'll have to go and make a phone call. But I shan't be leaving the village, Mrs. Cummins. I'll come straight back.'

'Any idea when we can expect the happy event?' the woman's husband asked.

'Around midnight, I think, but one can't really tell, you know. I shall know more in an hour, perhaps.'

Kay took her leave and walked to the telephone box. It wasn't very far but, even so, she felt weary as she lifted the receiver. The intense concentration which she had needed to drive to Kilbernian had taken more out of her than she realized, especially after the physically and emotionally exhausting nine hours which had already passed.

Margaret answered the phone at the other end and immediately sensed the tiredness in Kay's voice.

'Are you all right, dear?' she asked anxiously.

'I'm fine; just a bit tired, that's all. The drive was worse than I had expected. I called to see if there had been any calls since I left.'

'No, none,' her aunt replied. 'Look, Kay, how long are you likely to be in Kilbernian?'

'A few hours, I should imagine. Why do you ask?'

'I'm worried about you. You are going to be much too tired to drive back after the delivery. Would you like me to ask Clive to come and fetch you? You can always collect your car tomorrow.'

Relief flooded through Kay at this suggestion. She knew that she would find the drive home again very arduous, especially if the confinement was to be a long one. 'Oh, Aunt, has Clive come home? I must say I should be very grateful if he would come and collect me.'

'Yes, he came in a short while ago. Wait a moment — I'll call him to the phone, then you can ask him yourself.'

'All right — and thank you.' Kay tensed herself as she waited. She felt suddenly reluctant to speak to Clive for fear of what he might have to say to her. He had promised to explain everything to her when she had seen him that morning, but that seemed so far away now and so much had happened in between. She sighed heavily as she hung on, and she fancied she could hear his footsteps approaching. She pictured the hall, and a sad smile touched her face. She wished Frank Munro had never come to Stranduthie, for that was when their troubles had started. The next moment, the receiver at the other end was picked up, and then Clive spoke.

'Kay, are you all right? Margaret has just told me that you'd like me to collect you. Where are you calling from? What's the situation?'

He sounded so concerned that she fancied for a moment everything was still the same between them. Tears came to her eyes as she began to explain what had happened, but he cut her short after getting the gist of it.

'Look, Kay, I don't know what's been happening over the past few days. You've been run off your feet and so have I. Munro didn't help matters either, coming here and leaving as he did. I'm on call tonight, obviously, but I'll come out now and talk to you. If your case isn't hotting up yet, we can get together, and I think I owe you an explanation.' He laughed rather harshly. 'Don't tell me that you haven't noticed the stresses of the past days.'

'I've noticed quite a lot,' she said unsteadily.

'Then give me half an hour and I should be with you. Will you do that?'

'Of course. I'll be at the Cummins's house.'

'Good. I'll come there for you.'

The line went dead then, and Kay replaced the receiver and walked slowly back to the home of her patient. She didn't know what to think, but there was a faint glimmer of hope in her heart.

There was nothing to do but wait. There were some hours yet before the case would be concluded, and usually, in such circumstances, Kay departed to return later. But now she waited for Clive to come and the Cummins couple made her very welcome. She sat in the bedroom with Mrs. Cummins, trying to keep the woman's mind occupied while the time dragged by, until Jock Cummins appeared to tell her that Clive had arrived.

Clive came into the room, although it

was rare for a doctor to see the patient before the child was born. Kay watched his face while he chatted with Mrs Cummins, and she felt that she would never be able to bear the pain of losing him. He smiled at her when he caught her eye.

'I'd like to talk to you, Nurse, for a few minutes,' he said finally. 'Would you come out to my car?'

'Certainly, Doctor!' She smiled as she got to her feet, and they left the house and went to his car.

Clive opened the door for her and she got thankfully into the warm interior of the vehicle. She thought of the woman who had occupied this seat several times in the past few days, and could not help wondering about her. Then Clive got into the car and switched on the interior light. He looked at her for some moments without speaking, and Kay watched his face intently, telling herself how much she loved him.

'I'm sorry about the past two days or

so,' he said at length. 'I hope you haven't thought I've been neglecting you.'

'We've all been rather busy,' she said lamely, and he nodded.

'I have Munro to blame for most of my problems,' he went on. 'I knew as soon as I saw that he was interested in you that I'd have trouble with him. I guessed what he would do, and I was right.'

'I don't understand, Clive,' Kay said slowly.

'Of course not, but you will when I explain. Knowing Munro so well, I did what I hoped would forestall him.' He drew a sharp breath. 'How can I put it? I don't want to tell a long story that would probably bore you, anyway. Munro always accused me of taking away from him the girl he planned to marry. He would never listen to reason about that — he always had too much pride and he could never accept that she just didn't want to marry him. She used me as an excuse, I'll admit, and I got something of a reputation that I didn't deserve. It affected my career a lot more than I thought it might, but that's all water under the bridge now. I'm quite happy in my present situation.'

'How does all this affect us?' Kay demanded impatiently.

'When Munro decided that he wanted to get to know you better, despite the fact that we seemed to be going out together, he did what I imagined he would do because it was so characteristic of him. He got in touch with the girl who had caused all my trouble, to tell her I was here. He didn't know that we had parted amicably some long time ago — he thought I had run out on her. However, she knows Munro as well as, if not better than, I, and she warned me what Munro was up to and also informed someone else of Munro's whereabouts. Munro has played a lot of shabby tricks on a number of people, and when this person arrived here two days ago,

Munro decided to quit cold, which is what he did today. Am I making myself clear?'

'I think so,' Kay said doubtfully. 'I don't really know. You have explained some things that puzzled me, but I don't understand about Munro. He hoped that this girl would show up here and cause more trouble for you, is that it?'

'Perfectly!' Clive smiled. 'He thought I would do what I did the last time, and that was pack my bags and turn my back upon a highly promising career. But this other doctor turned up instead, and when I told Munro, it was he who decided to clear out.'

'So you knew he was going?'

'No. I thought he might. I arranged a meeting for him today with the doctor — there was the question of some missing money, among other things — but Munro didn't turn up to meet the doctor, and by the time I got home to check on him he had flown.'

'I see,' Kay paused. There was still

the unknown woman to account for, but Kay knew she could not bring herself to broach the subject. Clive would have to bring it up himself.

'You're not entirely happy, are you?' Clive demanded, peering into her face. 'What else is worrying you, Kay?'

She considered for a moment, trying to think up an excuse. Then her uncle came to mind.

'I'm worried about Uncle Edgar,' she said slowly. 'He came home earlier fairly worn out by the shock of Frank's departure.'

'I know, and that's why I was in a quandary over Munro. But, as it is, everything has worked out for the best. This doctor who came to see Munro hasn't a position anywhere at the moment. When I said there was a locum's job going begging here, she asked if she could be considered for it.'

'She?' Kay said wonderingly.

'Yes!' Clive stared at her with a frown on his face. 'You didn't think Munro could work his wiles on a man, did you?

It's a woman doctor. I had the devil of a job keeping her from going for Munro tooth and nail when she arrived, but, mercifully, I managed to talk her out of all thoughts of revenge, and she feels that by chasing Munro out of his job here and replacing him she has exacted vengeance of a sort. So everyone seems to be happy.'

'Everyone!' Kay sighed deeply. Her mind was buzzing with speculation. 'Was it the woman doctor you were lunching with today at the hotel?'

'Yes!' He frowned again. 'I arranged for Munro to meet her there for lunch, and when I called in to see if he had arrived I found that he hadn't. But how did you know about that?'

'It doesn't matter!' Kay blinked back her sudden tears of relief 'But there is still one question I would like to know the answer to, Clive.'

'What's that?'

'Do you love me?'

He smiled as he slid along the seat towards her, and the next moment she was in his arms; his breath was warm against her cheek. She looked up into his face, and saw a smile on his lips.

'I love you, Kay,' he said vibrantly. 'You shouldn't have to ask me that, you know. But I was getting worried — you've seemed so remote these past few days. I thought that Munro was having some effect upon you.'

'No,' she said softly. 'I never knew he existed. I love only you, Clive.'

'Then it must have been my imagination,' he retorted, and she nodded slowly as he kissed her . . .

When she opened her eyes, Kay saw snowflakes sticking to the windows of the car, and she shivered and stirred, withdrawing from his arms.

'Duty calls,' she said regretfully.

'It does most of the time,' Clive replied, 'but we're going to make time for ourselves in future, Kay. There's plenty of time for duty and a time for love.'

Kay clung to him, her mind looking ahead to that future, and she knew with full certainty that it had never seemed brighter. This was all she wanted, all she had ever hoped for, and she knew this was only the beginning . . .

Other titles in the
Linford Romance Library:

WISHES CAN COME TRUE

Angela Britnell

Meg Harper is shocked when the man she knows as Lucca Raffaele, who stood her up in Italy the previous summer, arrives to stay at her family home in Tennessee — this time calling himself her step-cousin, Jago Merryn . . . Jago is there to acquire a local barbecue business, but discovering the woman who came close to winning his heart is only one of the surprises in store for him. Can they move past their mistrust and seize a second chance for their wishes to come true?

CHRISTMAS TREES AND MISTLETOE

Fay Cunningham

The idea of another family Christmas fills Fran with dread, particularly when she is asked to pick up her mother's latest charity case and bring him along. But Ryan Conway is not what she was expecting. He is looking after his young niece while his sister is in hospital, and Fran decides the pair of them may not be such bad company after all. Then, once the festivities are in full swing, Santa arrives unexpectedly — and Fran's life changes forever . . .